THE CAVE OF SHADOWS

Martyn Rhys Vaughan

Published by
Llyfrau Cambria Books, Wales, United Kingdom.
*Cambria Books is a division of
Cambria Publishing.*
Discover our other books at: www.cambriabooks.co.uk

To James and Owain.
Two men who are not afraid to go where
science leads.

"All shadows whisper of the sun."
Emanuel Carnevali

Cover design by Ainsley Rees

CONTENTS

PROLOGUE

Four men sat in the central area of a vast yurt in the village of Interlaken in what had once been Switzerland. From various sites in the area one could admire the mighty peaks of the Eiger, Monck and Jungfrau, now utterly devoid of snow and ice. Of course, no-one referred to them by those names anymore. The old names given by the Degenerates had been swept away and replaced by honorifics of the virile warlords who had carved out new realms from the festering corpse of the despised Old Ways.

The four men did not wish to waste time admiring mere slabs of rock and moraine: they had grander things to consider. They were in an ebullient mood – there was the feeling abroad that new conquests were in the offing; new peoples to conquer and enslave.

The four men were not from the highest ranks of the Protectorate: they were merely the rulers of medium-sized satraps. No, they had been chosen for their organising abilities and thus it was to them that the Great Khan had given the honour of carrying to completion this particular one of the many plans his fertile mind had produced. They knew that he would be bountiful if success should crown their endeavours. They, or their children, or their children's children would be given many gifts, including the selection of the choicest women from the ranks of the Degenerates.

Maroun spoke first.

'Well Korok, what is the current situation? Report.'

A large, heavy-boned man gave a smile that somehow portrayed menace and said 'All is well. Our army grows stronger by the day.' Korok's deep voice conveyed the feeling of great rocks grinding together.

Gang Jianguo gave him a sharp look from hooded eyes.

'Fine words Korok but this is not a matter for levity or overconfidence. Our people long once again to feel the scimitar in their hands. Without opponents, without enemies to crush, they will grow soft. The vices of the Degenerates will once again take root and grow, eventually dimming and draining the virility of our warriors.'

His voice rose to a strong timbre and he once again recited his favourite quote:

' "*Man's greatest fortune is to chase and defeat his enemy, seize his possessions, leave his married women weeping and wailing, ride his gelding, use the bodies of his women as night-shirts and supports, gazing upon and kissing their rosy breasts, sucking their lips which are as sweet as the berries of their breasts.*" '.

The others showed their appreciation of the famous words by beating their thighs with their palms and then after their display of approval had subsided, Rocha nodded.

'Pity, compassion, forgiveness will rise again. The morality of the slave, the deceits of the prisoner who begs for compassion so he can avoid the sharp steel of his master's wrath, will fester and spread. Those days of grovelling cowardice must not return. Those so-called men who in their filth became little better than women; who indeed in the end wanted to become like women and grow breasts and give suck.'

The group of four almost shuddered at that grotesque image and tried to put aside all thoughts of the unutterable crimes of the Degenerates.

Maroun brought the meeting back to order and nodded to Gang to continue his questioning.

'Your people – is their obedience total? Can they be trusted in all things?'

Korok gave another of his fearful smiles. The other three were unmoved: they were not afraid of smiles.

'They are mine to command in all things,' he said in his

firm, powerful voice, 'I could cast a trinket into the furnace and order them to retrieve it and they would not hesitate. They are mine.'

'I take you to mean that they belong to the Great Khan,' Maroun corrected, 'He hears everything and will not tolerate prideful arrogance in inferiors.'

Korok bowed his head; his face as penitential as he could make it.

'I am a humble minion in the Protectorate,' he assured the others, 'If the Great Khan threw a trinket into the furnace and commanded me to retrieve it I would do so.'

The others appeared to be mollified.

'And when do you begin?'

'In four weeks.'

'And you are ready to accompany them?'

Korok risked a smile again.

'I am. I will be the Great Khan's eyes and ears. And if necessary, his fatal scimitar.'

Maroun seemed satisfied at last.

'It is approved. You shall be their leader. You shall be he who wields the scimitar of the Great Khan. Go Korok – greatness awaits your spirit.'

Korok rose, bowed and left the central area to meet their very different destinies.

THE WORLD OF SHADOWS
Part One

One

Jon could not quite remember when he had first begun to wonder if there was something wrong with The Universe. It had lain at the bottom of his mind like a sleeping worm for a long time: now it was beginning to stir and rise to the mind's hitherto calm surface. There *was* something wrong with the world - but what was it?

He looked around: things were as he remembered them – lush, tropical foliage, heavily bedewed with the recent thunderous downpour; tree ferns swaying slightly in a gentle breeze and rising up, up in mighty wooden columns; the akaro trees, rising so high that Jon thought that they must puncture the great crimson sky itself.

Everything seemed normal; as it should be – but there was that worm, that worm that whispered in his ear: *This is not right. Things are not as they should be. You must remember.*

Jon shrugged mentally: this was not helping him catch a meal. He knew the world of moving things was divided sharply into two types: the six-footed things that usually ran away from him into the forest and he, himself, the only creature that walked on two legs and (occasionally) spoke.

Now was one of those times.

'Come on Jon – this is no time for dreaming. This won't catch a kabarra.'

But he stopped again and sat down heavily on a fallen log.

Jon.

That was his name – but how had he known that? Why should he be called anything? There was no-one to call that name; no-one for him to answer to.

Why should he have a name?

He shook his head as if trying to throw off the cobwebs that were clouding his brain. These thoughts – he had not had them yesterday – why should he have them today? Why only yesterday –

He stopped.

What about yesterday?

He suddenly realised that he could not remember anything that had happened yesterday; it was if there had never been a yesterday; as if he had sprung fully formed into this world. A cold shiver of fear swept up his spine and he hung on to the log to stop himself falling.

This was madness – he was going mad. Of course, there had been a yesterday, just like there would be a tomorrow and a day after that.

This had to stop! He jerked himself upright and reached for his throwing stick. Somewhere there would be something to eat.

It was getting hotter slowly so it must be near the midpoint of the time of light. Then would come the time of darkness when he would become the prey if he was still on the ground. He had wasted enough time! With a new determination, he sent the worm of doubt back down into his subconscious and banished all those crazy doubts.

Food! That must be his only thought from now on. Somehow he knew that it would not be too long before the time of darkness.

He looked closely at the moist black soil that his bare feet were pressing into, searching for tracks. There must be a kabarra nearby; they were not uncommon.

With a steady purpose he pressed further into the undergrowth, heedless of the thorns that struck across his exposed flesh. He was dressed only in a loincloth that covered the lower third of his torso; a brown, tightly muscled physique that clearly displayed visible ridges of hard strength.

As he walked slowly and carefully through the dense

6

undergrowth his ears were on alert for the high-pitched chattering that indicated the presence of a kabarra troupe.

Nothing as yet – he felt a little spasm of worry. He must eat soon!

He looked up into the crimson sky which was visible only in segments through the canopy of the akaro trees: already purple bands were beginning to appear in it; a sure sign of the approach of the time of darkness.

Then he stopped and his whole body froze into a powerful rigidity: he heard them – a distant chattering coming from directly ahead. He was near to a troupe.

Instantly he lowered himself so he was as close to the moist ground as he could get and, gripping the throwing stick in the business position, he crept stealthily forward.

No big cat could have moved more noiselessly, more unobtrusively, as did Jon that day as he zeroed in on his unseen quarry. Then the undergrowth suddenly terminated and there, in a little clearing with the red light slanting down onto them in a cascade of crimson, were the kabarras; an entire family of them – adults of all three sexes and a gang of infants happily tumbling over each other in a mad melee of innocent play.

Jon knew he could not advance further into the clearing without alerting the family group to his presence. As misfortune would have it, the creatures were at the far end of the space at the limit of his throwing range. He could not aim for the infants because they were moving far too fast as they fell over and under their playmates in their dizzying games. It would have to be one of the adults. A pity – they were far tougher on the teeth.

Knowing he had one chance and one only, he drew back his stick and threw. It seemed to take an eternity to cross the distance between Jon and the creatures; he almost believed he could walk leisurely alongside it as it crawled across the intervening space.

But it hit one of the adults squarely in the neck. It gave a pitiful squeak and collapsed. The infants stopped their play and rushed up to it, nuzzling it as they gave little whimpering sounds. The display of grief ended abruptly as their keen ears detected Jon's approach and, as one, the infants and the remaining adults swung round to face him, emerald eyes flashing, emerald teeth gleaming.

At first Jon thought they were going to rush him but then their natural cowardice took hold and with one last squeal of defiance they disappeared into the undergrowth. Jon was left to examine the dead kabarra at his leisure. He held it up by its tail at arm's length to make sure it was really deceased: kabarra teeth are not only green but very sharp.

It took him only a moment to realise that his kill was of the onari sex, not the more desirable male or female. Just his luck! Onaris are notoriously tough and stringy.

Sitting down on the springy black vegetation he gave the creature a minute examination to check for any sign of disease or external parasites. Fortunately, there were none but as he studied the animal he wondered for the first time why the middle set of legs was so vestigial. What was the point of having six legs if two of them didn't even reach the ground?

It was a puzzle beyond his ability or interest, Jon rapidly decided. He was not responsible for designing the things, only for eating them. And to that end he took the kabarra in both hands and with a sudden jerk of his muscular arms broke it in two. The creature's insides were homogenous; a solid mass of brownish material with the consistency of a particularly well-set jelly. Using his fingers Jon scooped out a handful of the tough but very delicious stuff and spend the next time period thoroughly cleaning out the creature until all that was left was the head and an empty skin which he threw away into the undergrowth where tiny six-legged things suddenly appeared, from apparently nowhere, and began devouring it.

8

Finally, he stood up, feeling immensely stronger and more optimistic with a full belly. Some of that optimism left him however, as he caught a glimpse of the sky above him which was no longer obscured by overarching trees. In the clearing, the sky was beautifully framed in a circular colonnade of mighty trunks which gave it the appearance of a glowing dome. But that dome was now criss-crossed with ominous bars of purple which now took up over half the apparent area: the time of darkness was upon him.

Jon was angry with himself – he had spent too long devouring every morsel of the kabarra; he should have just contented himself with the softer part and not indulged himself. Now he was in danger!

He had to get off the ground into the comparative safety of the akaro canopy but that would be difficult for their trunks are very smooth and slippery with the canopy only appearing at a daunting elevation.

He must do it!

He looked around at the mighty colonnade of trees, searching for some way up, some way off this ground which would soon become a fatal arena of death. Then he saw his escape route – an old akaro had partly fallen and was resting against the side of a healthy neighbour. He could use the slope of the fallen trunk to get some way up the tree before he needed to start climbing.

Quickly now, quickly!

Stowing his throwing stick into a fold of his loin cloth he sprinted for the fallen tree trunk. Even as he did so the whole forest shuddered to the sound of a deep, powerful roar that sent the needle-like leaves of the akaros trembling, as if with well-merited fear.

Jon did not bother trying to clamber up the sloping trunk but ran up it, his bare feet somehow gripping its smooth surface. Then he leapt off the fallen bole as it met the still living tree and grasping both sides of that trunk began to inch himself up. Akaros get less smooth as one ascends but the lower part was hideously slippery. Time and again Jon though he was safe only to find himself sliding down again to the doom that awaited him on the forest floor.

There was another roar – louder, nearer, more terrifying. Still he clung to the mirror-like bark, trying to ascend. He calmed his raging mind: panic was not helping. He must abandon his wild efforts to ascend and think his approach through – or pay the price.

Desperately trying not to slide back down to where he had started he finally noticed that a patch of the trunk some distance above him and to the right was rougher than the rest. He must not rush; that would only send him sliding downwards again, but carefully – oh so carefully! – he must slowly ascend until his hands could reach that patch.

He pressed his feet onto the bark, trying to use his toenails to get more purchase, and, trying not to think about how long all this was taking, he gradually, gingerly, approached the area of bark that would save him.

He reached it and found that he could ascend more than the distance he had already travelled in a fraction of the time. Soon he had reached the first branch; a mighty structure that crossed a good third of the width of the clearing. Utterly drained, he lay full length on the branch, his arms hanging down either side of it and his face flat against its smooth surface. As he did so the entire sky went purple and an instant later jet black. The time of darkness fell like a great ebon cloak over the forest and all the chattering tree denizens became instantly silent. Jon lay there, not moving, not caring.

Time passed in the dark, featureless silence. Nothing happened. Nothing moved.

Jon finally lifted his head and looked carefully to the left and right. And then down.

And there it was – a great black shape, hardly visible except as a darkness greater than the surrounding darkness. A living darkness that somehow radiated a feeling of power and menace. The dark mass at the end of the greater darkness moved. It was a great head and as it moved Jon could see it was looking up into the tree, for two great viridian eyes became visible; great saucer eyes with shone not by reflected light, for there was none, but by a baleful inner power that cast shadows onto the hitherto unseen surroundings. It saw Jon and roared. The roar had been powerful enough at some distance but now it was so close that the great tree literally shook like a sapling. Despite the risk of falling Jon was forced to clasp his ears to keep out that awful noise.

And then came the noise of scrabbling claws and Jon could see the thing was trying to ascend the tree to reach him. Six strong taloned feet bit into the bark and very, very slowly it started to climb.

Jon stared at it as it silently approached. There was nowhere to run. He hadn't the strength to try to climb higher and even if he did, his progress would be so slow that the thing would easily be able to rear up and claim him.

There was only one chance and there would be only one opportunity to take that chance. Jon had never been so close to one of these killers before but he had seen dead ones and remembered something of their anatomy. This was no time to doubt his memories.

Relentlessly the predator came on, its clawed feet making its ascent much swifter than Jon's laboured climb. He could hear the clash as chitinous jaws snapped together, gradually getting louder and more terrifying. In a moment its head would appear above the branch and then would be the instant for this one, this only chance. Jon was ready. He drew back his arm and tensed the hand that held the throwing stick. Already he could smell its breath. Any moment now. Any moment.

The head appeared above the branch, bathing Jon in a horrible putrid glow of green death, two saucer eyes staring at him, mocking him, telling him "You are mine!"

Two saucer eyes.

And then there was one as Jon thrust his stick into the nearer eye, pulled it out and thrust it at the second orb. He missed but the creature pulled back and, losing its grip, flailed its upper four limbs and then lost its footing completely and tumbled back down. As it hit the ground it roared again in a sonic explosion so great that Jon thought his skull would explode.

Silence came in a great wave of peace, crashing over the trees and its one four-limbed inhabitant. Jon decided to dare to look down to see if the wounded creature was returning to claim him, to seek horrific revenge for its maiming.

But it had gone.

Jon lay there on the branch, not daring to sleep for fear of tumbling to the ground into jaws that were assuredly waiting for him. Eventually, he became aware of a faint purplish glow around him and the trees gradually emerged from their cloak of blackness.

A new time of light was dawning.

He was safe for the moment. The predators only came out during the time of darkness. Carefully, he rose so he was sitting on his heels before attempting the perilous return to the forest floor. As he did so, his eyes came level with a gap in the canopy through which he could see a distant hill.

And from that hill rose a thin blue column of what other observers would have interpreted as smoke.

What could that mean? Jon had never seen smoke in this rain-sodden wilderness and so was unable to put a name, rightly or wrongly, to what he saw. And yet he had a feeling that it meant something tremendously important.

Something he would have to investigate and learn its secret.

Carefully, he began his return to the surface.

12

Two

Jon made steady progress through the resistant undergrowth, making sure that he kept his bearing on that distant hill which was now hidden again by the sweeping curtains of black vegetation. Sometimes he could climb onto a pile of fallen tree trunks to see if he could see its dim outline and its enigmatic column of bluish substance. Usually, it was obscured by the riotous mass of fervent vegetation but sometimes he could catch a glimpse of it; apparently as distant as ever.

As he trudged through the seemingly endless mass of growing things he wondered again and again why he was doing this. It must be a pointless drain on his limited energy reserves. Would there be more kabarras there? It seemed unlikely as they were creatures of the jungle and as far as he could see the hill was only lightly clothed with vegetation.

Why was he doing it? He could not explain it to himself; it was as if there was some unconscious compulsion driving him on, forcing his complaining muscles to take step after step through the resisting bushes and scrub, a compulsion that made him heedless of the slashing thorns that seem to impede every step.

At last, he could drive his weary legs no more and he crashed down on a fallen log.

'By Korok, I've had enough of this!' he roared at the crimson sky, clenching his fists in impotent anger.

He paused: why had he said that? He had never said that meaningless expression before. What did it mean?

What was a "Korok"?

Another mystery and he was getting very tired of mysteries. Only yesterday (if there had indeed been a yesterday) he had had no experience of mysteries. Surely his life had been a simple one

13

with only two imperatives – Firstly, hunt and eat kabarras; Secondly, avoid being eaten by the great night predators. What else did life have to offer? It must be impossible that there could be anything else.

And yet – there was that nagging worm that kept whispering that something was not right, that there was some great hidden secret that had not yet been revealed to him; some secret that he would have to look for and discover.

He sat there for a while with his head in his hands. It was all too much for so simple a man as he. Why could he not simply accept the world for what it was? There was only one world and this was it. There were the great trees, the scuttling kabarras, the night predators; all carrying out their existence under the great crimson sky. There was nothing else. How could there be? Outside of Everything there is only Nothing.

Finally, he realised that he was wasting valuable time before the time of darkness came again. He cast an anxious glance at the sky and was relieved to see that as yet there were no lurid bars of purple crisscrossing its featureless surface. There was no immediate danger. Then he noticed something that he had not realised until then: the trees were thinning out. There were definitely fewer of them than he was used to. How could he escape a night predator should one stalk him in the coming dark period?

It must be literal madness to continue, he told himself angrily. He must stop. Or at the very least find some shelter from the predators which even now must be gradually emerging from their day-time sleep.

He could now get a better view of that enigmatic hill and now that it was hardly obscured by vegetation he could see that it was unquestionably nearer. Straining his eyes, Jon could see there appeared to be a cluster of structures encircling its flat summit, from the centre of which arose that thin bluish smoke-like column. He felt gratified that his labours seemed to have had

14

some effect.

He studied the hill again. It was very odd. All the landscape around it was flat; geometrically flat. The actual surface he had been walking on was hidden by the growing things, and all the akaro trees rose to almost exactly the same height, forming a black lid on top of the ground, so he was unable to decide whether the land suddenly became flat or not. The trees were mostly behind him now; ahead they petered out and were replaced by a gradually thinning expanse of scrub, dotted with clumps of boulders.

Because of the supreme flatness of its surroundings, the hill was in all probability not as high as it appeared. Jon had no experience of elevations other than the trees and had no way of estimating just how high it was. The hill was also surprisingly regular, almost perfectly cone-like in its dimensions, with what looked like a precisely flat top. It was in fact a good approximation of a frustum – although Jon was innocent of that word.

Despite all his misgivings he decided to press on. Perhaps he could reach the hill before the time of darkness.

Then an amazing thought struck him, a thought so profoundly astounding that he gave a little grunt of wonderment.

Those structures near the top of the elevation – could there be things like him – Jon – there? Could there be more of him in this Universe – more Jons?

It was a truly staggering idea. He had no idea how such a ridiculously outlandish thought could have come to him. He had always thought he knew the Universe. There were night predators, kabarras, akaro trees, soil, stones and – him. Why should there be anything else? How *could* there be anything else?

Now that the thought had erupted, fully formed, into his mind he felt more determined than ever to reach that hill. He felt a strange certainty that somehow it held answers to these questions that had made these days so strange and bewildering.

With a fresh determination, he struck out into the scrub, leaving the last akaro tree behind him. He felt a strange sense of vulnerability, of a kind of nakedness as he left the forest farther and farther behind. In all his memories, he had never had so much almost empty space around him; there had always been the closeness of the growing things, the great grey gloom cast by the trees; the bushes that tore and impeded his progress. It was almost as if he was floating in a void, cut off from all he had known.

Perhaps things would be better when he was on top of that hill, surrounded by whatever those structures were.

He pressed on. Occasionally he cast a backward glance at the black wall of the forest but as that wall shrank down into a thin line he decided it was too unsettling to see his normal world reduced to insignificance. He decided to rest at a group of boulders that reached up quite a height towards the sky. He didn't like looking at that sky: there was simply too much of it. Instead of strips of reddish light between the branches there was just one enormous, unblemished dome that seemed to be sucking him upwards, drawing him into a great glowing crimson maw. He had kept his gaze low from then on.

He leaned against the nearest boulder; a great slab of pitted, greyish rock that bore a few films of some kind of barely alive plant.

He realised then that his exertions had given him a terrible thirst. The kabarra flesh had held some water but most of its constituent liquids had been various thick oils. Normally, he would simply break off a branch and suck the moisture out of it but here there was no vegetation large enough to have that kind of branch.

He looked around with growing desperation. Without water, he could not complete his trek and if he attempted to return to the forest, he would arrive at the same time as the darkness and be easy prey for the night creatures. Not for the

16

first time, he cursed the strange compulsion that had come over him and which now looked like bringing him to a premature end. Then on the harsh winds that were playing over his semi-nude body, he detected a familiar odour: the scent of water. Only those who are not short of that lifegiving liquid believe that it is odourless – to those in desperate need it has the sweetest, most wonderful odour imaginable. And Jon knew that it could not be far distant and lay in front of him, not behind.

He set off, imbued with a new spirit of confidence; almost of adventure. This new land was one he would conquer and make his own.

That spirit did not last too long as the ground before him became steadily stonier, more barren and less and less likely to hold any water. A heat haze started to ripple across the more distant vistas, giving false hope that there was indeed standing water not too far away.

Jon cursed his luck using the only curse he knew, the meaningless word that had come to him suddenly, not too long ago.

And then in the rippling distance he saw something that he had never seen before. On a ridge some unguessable distance away were three stick-like objects. At first Jon thought that they were dead trees, rearing leafless branches to the sky. But no! – he saw that they were moving. They were walking upright – like he himself. One question had been answered: there were indeed creatures like him in The Universe. He was not alone!

A wave of previously unknown emotion powered through him then. Others! There was a word which suddenly meant something.

Companionship. He would be able to interact with beings like himself but not himself. It was such an alien concept that for a moment he felt unsteady and had to lean against a rock to avoid collapsing. Would they look exactly like him? (He had no real idea of his appearance as there were no bodies of standing water of any size anywhere in the forest.) Would they be able to speak and if so, would he understand them?

The whirl of sudden possibilities was almost overwhelming. Kabarras he could deal with, the night predators he knew how to avoid – but things like him? The unknown possibilities were almost frightening.

But one thing was sure – if he did not meet up with them he would never know. He raised his spinning head from his chest and looked again where he had seen them.

They were gone.

* * *

Jon carried on further into the wilderness, wondering more and more if he was wandering into his doom. But the compulsion would not let him go; like an animal caught in the jaws of a larger beast, he could not change his direction.

And then he found it. Cresting a low ridge, he came across a still expanse of what must be water. It was streaked through with black scum but between the tendrils of that growth he could see the red light reflecting off what could only be a liquid.

Carefully he approached it. If it was indeed water it was the largest body of that substance he had ever seen. There was water aplenty in the forest but it was bound up in the soil and could only be seen as droplets when that substance was compressed by hands or feet. Here it miraculously formed a pool so large that Jon could not have jumped across it. Large indeed. He bent down to investigate it more fully. There were long strips of slime winding their way just under the surface and hordes of tiny black things darting so rapidly over the surface that he could not get a clear view of them. But by carefully angling his interlinked hands into the water he was able to get a sufficient amount to drink and which only contained one or two of the little darting things. The water was warm and had a greasy undertaste which the water from the bushes did not have, but in Jon's parched state it was the sweetest nectar.

Ignoring the faint wrigglings of the little black things as they disappeared into his digestive tract, Jon looked around with reinvigorated vision. The land was not becoming any more welcoming; quite the opposite in fact. He arose to get a better view of the mysterious hill when he noticed something on the ground. Or rather *in* the ground for he saw a number of shallow oval depressions.

They could be footprints he decided, putting his own feet next to them. The ground was too hard to give any indication of toes or footwear but the way they were spaced gave a clear indication that something had been striding along next to this pool. The indentations were about the same size as his own feet, which was further proof.

A thrill passed through him. The prints must have been made by the other Jons that he had seen in the distance. He had not imagined them and they must be near! Soon he would meet them and be able to finally have companions in this dreadful world!

Just then he realised that the light from the sky had taken a dull carnelian tint that was rapidly transmuting into an ominous purple cast.

The time of darkness!

One glance at the sky was all the confirmation he needed. Several purple bands had appeared and were stretching from horizon to horizon. He looked around in increasing concern for a place of refuge.

All he could see were the various piles of boulders, scattered randomly over the austere terrain. He sprinted towards the highest of the nearer ones and with panic starting to throb through him scrabbled his panting way to the top. He knew that this pile of rubble was not as high as an akaro tree but it was his only chance.

Just as he reached the top all light vanished instantly as if a switch had been thrown. He lay there, his heart hammering, waiting for sounds of movement and the terrifying roars.

Nothing happened for quite some time and then he heard them – the unmistakeable cries of the night predators. But they were so far away, so faint and only coming from the direction of the forest. Gradually the joyful realisation came to him: the predators were confined to the forest – there were none out here in this rocky wilderness!

He lay on his back, feeling the tension in his body fade as muscle and sinew relaxed. He found himself staring up at an enormous sky, much, much bigger than the one he was accustomed to, for here there was no intervening vegetation to block the view. He looked deep into it, finding it impossible to shake the feeling that he was looking down into a vast bottomless sea of inky nothingness. Were there any lights in that sea, any sign of other existences?

He stared long and hard. There was nothing; just blackness piled high on blackness. Nothing.

Eventually his exhausted body demanded its rest and he drifted, unknowingly, into a deep sleep.

And so it was that in his sleep he did not hear the faint sounds of movement in the darkness below him.

Three

The crepuscular light gave Jon's surroundings a weird mauve tint as he gradually returned to consciousness. He stretched his arms and back to drive out the stiffness which had invaded them during the unaccustomed cold of the time of darkness; such times were not as bitter in the forest because of the comforting cloak of the vegetation.

Gradually strength and agility returned to his powerful frame and he dropped lightly to the stony ground. He stood with his back against the pile of rocks and slowly scanned his surroundings. Above him the sky slowly became a more dramatic scarlet from its initial pale cerise. Despite the excitement he still felt about the possibility of companions he had not lost his alertness and his mistrust of apparently peaceful surroundings. Many times in the forest he had gone from peace to peril in an instant and he had not forgotten those lessons. Perhaps the new Jons that he was about to meet lead a quieter life; perhaps out here on the stony plains there were fewer dangers. It was a pleasant, almost intoxicating thought. To one side he could see the black wall of the forest; shrunken now to a one-dimensional line. Ahead and off to one side stood the enigmatic hill that was his ultimate destination, now much closer than in his initial view but still disappointingly distant.

He was about to resume his seemingly interminable journey when he noticed that the ground around his refuge had been disturbed since he had last seen it. There were new oval depressions in the ground, which he interpreted as showing that one or more of the new Jons had passed close to him in the time of darkness. Why hadn't he heard them and woken up, he groaned inwardly, now it would be an unknown period before he had the chance again!

21

He tried to follow the line of tracks but the ground was too hard and he soon lost them among the stone and gravel that was this area's equivalent of the rich dark soil that he had known in the forest. He decided to abandon the attempt; if he was correct in interpreting the objects at the top of the hill as dwellings then surely there must be Jons living in them. All he had to do was complete his quest and at last he would have the companionship that he longed so much for.

His mind made up, he took one last look at his resting place and struck out for the hill.

The time of light drew on and the temperature began to climb. Once again heat hazes started to ripple and dance in the distance, mocking the eyes with their appearance of running water. He was not dismayed: he had found water once – he would find it again.

Then far off on one of the tawny ridges that were apparently endless in this area, he saw one of the stick figures again. He stopped his march to study the thing, to ensure that heat and wishful thinking were not deceiving him. He stood alertly motionless and watched. Yes, it was definitely moving – it was indeed one of the new Jons.

Although the figure was not in the direct line to the hill he veered off his course and quickened his pace so he could intercept the figure and bring this mystery to a satisfactory conclusion. He climbed up and over ridges and around gigantic boulders, all the while keeping his gaze on the distant figure.

And so it was that as he came around one particularly colossal slab of stone that he did not immediately see them.

Then he did. And stopped.

Facing him were five figures. But they were not Jons.

They were tall with a spare angularity, their skins black and armoured. Spines stood out from their arms and shoulders and their eyes were crystals of a substance that gleamed like rubies in the red light from the sky. They had six limbs; two were

22

employed as legs and the others as arms, although the lower two were so small that they were almost vestigial.

And they bore spears and axes. Spears and axes of sharp, mirror-smooth blackness that seemed to take the crimson light into them and destroy it. Jon himself was dark-skinned but this blackness was unreal, unnatural, like looking through a hole in reality into another universe.

He was so astounded by this totally unexpected development that he stood completely motionless staring at the eldritch apparitions. His mind whirled in crazy patterns. Should he run? Should he attack? Should he...

The nearest creature looked down on him and spoke.

Its voice was like a wind blowing sand off the barren ridges; thin and whispery and ominous.

'Do not move,' it said, 'or we will kill you.'

* * *

Jon could not tell how long they had been marching; he only knew that the route that they were taking was at right angles to the path to the hill. And that made him angry. Nothing was more important than getting to that hill – nothing!

'Where are you taking me?' he said for the third, or perhaps fourth, time.

As before there was no reply; ever since they had tied his hands behind him and put a rope around his neck there had been no communication. Three of the creatures marched behind him and two marched in front. They paid little attention to him except occasionally one of the ones behind would prod him with a goad if they thought he was too tardy. *Too tardy for what?* he wondered sourly, *where were they taking him and for what purpose?*

The first question was answered almost instantly. They came out of a maze of shattered rock and there before them was a group of huts surrounding an empty central area, which was

23

bounded by a low fence. The huts were conical and Jon noticed that the shape bore a striking resemblance in its angles to the hill that he had been trying to reach.

He was pulled and prodded into the little village and came to a halt just where the huts stopped and the empty central area began.

'This is where we will kill you,' the apparent leader observed matter-of-factly.

Jon stared up at the thing's face which was not only obsidian in hue but seemed to be carved out of actual obsidian. The ruby eyes stared back.

'Why do you want to kill me?' Jon demanded, 'what have I done?'

'That is a foolish question,' the leader replied in its thin, whispery tones, 'you have done nothing. We kill everything that comes out of the forest.'

'And how many like me have come out of the forest?'

'You are the first.'

Jon felt something sharp behind him and realised that his bonds were being cut off. Would there be a chance of escape?

He tried again. 'But why kill? Why not work together – to' - he searched for the word - 'co-operate?'

The leader approached and pulled the rope over Jon's head.

'More foolishness. It is The Law that we must strive and pit our strength against others. To struggle with all our strength and finally to conquer – that is The Law.'

Jon glanced angrily around with lidded eyes. No – too many – they had formed a tight circle about him, each within their long arm's length of him. So close that he could smell an acrid odour rising from their black bodies; it made him want to gag.

'This Law – who gave it to you?' he said, looking from emotionless face to emotionless face.

The leader placed a cold hand over Jon's lips. It was like having a reeking stone pressed into his face. He spluttered under

24

its pressure.

'You ask too many questions. We do not ask questions here. We do what is required and what is required is to follow The Law.'

'I don't even know who you are!' snapped Jon once the hand was removed. 'Why should I follow your Law!'

'We are the Lords of the Sands,' came the whispering reply. 'You need not know more as you will not be with us long.'

Jon gave up. The creatures were beyond reason. There was only one question left: could he take some of them with him into whatever lay beyond this mad Universe?

'How am I to die?' he finally asked.

The leader pointed to the smallest of the five captors.

'You will fight the weakest amongst us here in the place of death.' The leader pointed at the central space as he said those words.

Jon's eyes narrowed as he heard his sentence. *The weakest amongst them? There might be a way out!*

'And if I defeat your weakest?'

'You will fight the next weakest and so on until one is strong enough to overpower you. Then we will employ the Fatal Scimitar. It is an honour to have one's existence terminated by that wonder. It is made from our finest Midnight Steel.'

Jon stared at the group of dispassionate murderers which were encircling him and felt a strange new emotion boil up inside like magma searching for a vent to the splintering surface. The emotion was hatred. He had known fear before as he watched the night predator ascend the tree towards him. He had felt anger when his throwing stick had missed a fleeing kabarra. He had felt joy as he had ripped a young one apart and gorged himself on the tender meat.

But hatred? This was new.

Whatever it took these fiends would not find him a trembling victim. He was no kabarra. And "Fatal Scimitar" –

25

what did those words mean?

He tensed his muscular body and balled his fists.

'And when do we begin?'

'In the next time of light.'

As the leader uttered those words Jon realised that the light had already developed a purplish tinge.

Apparently, the ordeal was to be delayed.

Jon was taken into the nearest hut and fastened to the central pole. After some considerable time one of the Lords appeared carrying a flask and a shallow box. He left them on the floor of the hut within Jon's reach who picked up the box and examined its contents. The Lord waited while Jon did his study, seemingly interested to see what his reaction would be.

The box contained some plant leaves and a brown, leathery object, round at one end and tapering to a thin tendril at the other.

Jon looked up. 'What is this?'

'It is a root of the (unpronounceable) bush. It is nutritious to us. It may be nutritious to you.'

'You're feeding me even though you intend to kill me tomorrow.'

'Of course. Why should we wish to weaken you before combat? Our need is to test ourselves against strong adversaries, to know we have triumphed over a powerful and intelligent enemy. Anything else would be the way of the Degenerate.'

'I am not your enemy.'

'You are not one of us. Thus, you are our enemy.'

With that observation, the Lord terminated the conversation and strode out of the hut. Jon was left contemplating the root of the whatever-it-was bush. Knowing he had nothing to lose, he sank his teeth into it. It was tough, stringy and fibrous but he had had nothing to eat for a very long time and somewhat to his own surprise, he finished the entire thing.

The flask unsurprisingly contained water, a water which was

26

just as unpalatable and rancid as the water in the pool. But once again he had no choice and drained the contents.

He sat there, chained to the pole with no way of escape and considered his options.

That didn't take long as he didn't have any.

Unless he could defeat every Lord in this encampment he would surely die tomorrow.

How strong were they in actuality?

He sent his mind back to the moment of his capture. He had been so stunned that he had not put up much of a fight as they tied him up. How strong had they felt then?

Not for the first time Jon considered the fact that the creatures of this world didn't seem very well designed. Like the kabarras, these Lords had appendages that were apparently useless. Even the night predators hadn't seemed that efficient as hunters.

What did it all mean? He must figure it out.

He felt certain that he would not be able to sleep while he pondered these mysteries but to his amazement he found that his eyes had closed and that there was purple light slanting through the open door of the hut.

The time had come. The Fatal Scimitar awaited him.

Almost as soon as that thought had burned through his brain two Lords entered and roughly undid his chain. He was dragged into the rapidly intensifying light and brought before the one he recognised as the Leader.

'You will leave us now,' that individual observed helpfully, 'Here – this is your weapon.'

He handed Jon a blade of some wickedly sharp black ceramic that had been inserted into a skilfully carved handle.

Jon weighed it experimentally in his right hand. It was an excellent weapon, much better than his simple throwing stick. He glanced at the Leader – he was near enough for one killing up thrust.

The Leader read the message in his eyes. 'Killing me now would not avail. You would only ensure for yourself a dishonourable and extremely painful and protracted death. But you may well face me, should you kill my weaker brethren. Now no further delays.'

With that a wicker gate was opened and Jon was thrust into the central arena.

He looked around, keeping low to the ground like the hunted beast that he was.

A Lord, marginally smaller than the Leader, entered through a gate opposite him. He too was armed with the wicked killing knife.

The two circled each other, gazing into each other's faces. Jon was at an acute disadvantage for the only conflicts he had been involved with had been the death he handed out to fleeing kabarras, and they are not known for their ferocity.

Suddenly no more time for reflection. Like a bolt of jet lightning the Lord was on him, the knife sweeping up in an arc of death.

Jon leapt backwards, his forest-trained muscles doing the thinking for him, and his opponent swept past, carried by the momentum of its attack.

It turned in an instant and once again the knife carved through the unresisting air; this time making slashing contact with Jon's left forearm. A vivid red line instantly appeared as the flesh parted like paper and Jon felt a pain like molten metal pouring over his arm.

And this one's the weakest! he thought in his agony.

He fell backwards in his desperate haste to escape that ardent blade; staggered, catching one leg over the other and fell heavily to the sand.

Had the Lord had the facial muscles to smile sardonically at this point it would have done so but it did not, so it merely leaned forward to deliver the final blow.

28

As it did so Jon drove his own blade straight upwards into the centre of its chest and it was the Lord's flesh that parted like paper. There was a spray of perfectly white, milky liquid from the wound. The Lord dropped its knife and an instant later followed it to the wet, white-stained sand.

Jon stood up shakily, hardly able to believe that he had won.

The Lords, who had been watching from outside, raised their upper arms above their heads and gave out a booming ululation; whether in anger or appreciation, it was impossible to tell.

Jon was given some more of the tepid water and allowed to sit down for a short time. A very short time, for almost as soon as he had finished the water another opponent appeared on the other side of the arena and approached wielding a knife identical to the one Jon and his erstwhile opponent had carried.

Once again the combatants warily circled each other; once again suddenly making slashing or thrusting attacks with the instruments of death. To his surprise, Jon found that he was beginning to understand the tactics and techniques that the Lords were employing. Perhaps the creatures were not as clever as they obviously thought they were.

Just as he thought that, the other's blade came towards him out of nowhere and drew a scarlet line over Jon's bare chest. An instant later the blade came again and calmly flicked the knife out of Jon's hand. The Lord made a slight nodding motion of its grim head as if to say, "The contest is over" and moved forward.

In a relaxed manner, it came up to him and drew back the killing blade. For an instant their gazes locked and in that instant Jon seized the knife-wielding arm and bent it backward. The creature convulsed for a second and then Jon was suddenly behind it, bending the arm back and back, with another arm around its throat. The creature's vestigial arms scrabbled helplessly, trying to gain purchase on his sweat-soaked frame but failing to do so. It dropped the knife and, seizing the opportunity,

Jon put both of his mighty arms on the creature's head and gave a sudden powerful, twisting, irresistible jerk.

There was a loud "crack" and the Lord went limp in his grasp. Jon let its lifeless body slump to the sand. He turned to face the others. They had raised their upper arms and were making that weird howling which could be either approbation or fury.

And so the day wore on.

Opponent after opponent. Each stronger, more agile, wilier, more powerful than the previous. Jon's entire body became crisscrossed with dripping, scarlet lines, intersecting each other in a crazed pattern of death. The world became a blurred, crimson haze of hell in which ebony figures moved, slashing, probing, cutting. His legs became heavier and heavier while his mind became a misted thing, unable to plan, predict, tell the body to move out of the way of the stabbing bringer of oblivion.

And then it was all over. The knife dropped from fingers that could no longer grip, out of control of a mind that could no longer control.

He wanted it over. He had done far better than he had expected, lasted longer than he had any right to expect.

Now he could die, knowing that he had taken many with him. They would not be able to forget him very easily.

Let us end it now.

He fell to his knees, his head bowed.

He was vaguely aware that many of the Lords had gathered around him. Then the crowd parted and he thought he recognised the blurred figure of the Leader himself.

Slowly, agonisingly, he raised his head higher and forced his bloodshot eyes to focus.

It was the Leader. And it carried something. It was a curved blade, carved out of a strange black material. He had seen many shades of blackness before but nothing like this!

It was a blackness that should not exist, as if a Demiurge

30

God had forgotten to colour in all parts of his creation and left a hole through which another terrible universe could be glimpsed.

The Fatal Scimitar.

'You have done us a great service, stranger,' the distant voice whispered, 'many have tested themselves against you and you have rewarded them with a true challenge. Our people will be stronger for what you, our brave enemy, have accomplished. But your task here is done. Now you must leave us.'

It lifted the Fatal Scimitar.

Jon looked at those glowing rubies with no fear, only burning, esurient hatred.

'Do it!' he roared with the last shreds of his strength, 'By Korok, just do it!'

A great silence fell like an invisible cloak.

The Lords stood completely motionless.

Then the Leader spoke.

'Forgive us. We did not know that you had the power to speak the Holy Name. You are a warrior of the Great Lord. We should have known by your fighting spirit. Forgive us!'

And with that each Lord lowered itself to the sand and chanted: 'Forgive! Forgive!'

Four

Jon spent some time with the Lords of the Sands after his ordeal. They took him into the largest of the huts and applied many different types of salve to his crisscrossing wounds. The ointments stung and burned so badly that he let out many roars of pain. But they persisted and gradually the pain subsided. Then they bound the wounds with some type of plant fibre, much like linen, until there was hardly any flesh visible on his torso. His face, mercifully, had received few cuts.

They gave him several types of broth to eat and water that tasted almost fresh to wash down his meals. Then mostly they left him alone in the dim quiet of that hut to lie still and recover.

Jon was relieved to discover that they made no attempt to query him on his apparently exalted status. The fact that he had been able to utter the holy name without immediately being burned to a cinder was all the proof they needed, it seemed.

Jon himself avoided the topic in whatever short conversations he had with them for fear of revealing the fact that he had no idea who the Great Lord Korok was or which qualities that person possessed which made him so great.

Of the Lords of the Sands as a people, he learned nothing; mainly because they themselves knew nothing.

They had no history, no records of great deeds, of epic journeys or struggles going back into a deep and distant past. They might as well have snapped into existence yesterday. All that they knew, all that they lived for, was to fight and struggle and measure themselves against opponents. There were other tribes of Lords out there in the wilderness and on the few occasions when those tribes met there was always strife and violence.

Jon thought to himself that such an existence was utterly

meaningless but refrained from commenting. It looked as if that this was the whole sum of their culture, the core of their being and any disapproving opinions from him might push their trust of him to the limit. So he nodded wisely with the hint of a smile when they told him exultant tales of how they had come across a whole family of the others and slaughtered them all in their sleep.

Day by day, he tested his strength and resilience. It was a great day when he first managed to walk, haltingly, all the way around the encampment. The Lords seemed impressed by the speed of his recovery as well and took it as a further sign of his superior status.

Jon did not lose his hatred of them, however. He knew that he lived purely by a seemingly impossible chance; the chance that a single word, a single name, had somehow had the power to save him. He longed to see no more of these flint-like faces, the staring vermillion eyes, the spiny limbs, the cold whispers that were their voices.

And so the day came.

The bandages were removed and Jon looked down on his healed body. The salves had worked well and instead of red gashes he saw thin, spidery lines of white scar tissue. crossing his flesh in all directions. He ran his finger along one and was relieved to find that there was no pain.

All pain had gone and he felt invigorated, powerful.

For an instant, he toyed with the thought that perhaps he could now kill them all while they trusted him and were unprepared. But he put that thought away as unworthy: not that they did not deserve to die, but he was unwilling to be the agent of their destruction. He had killed several times under their tutelage and discovered that he did not enjoy it.

And so the day came when he was strong enough to leave the Lords of the Sands. They showed no emotion when he announced his departure - but then they never had. Even in

33

killing they had seemed entirely dispassionate. They gave him a short sword of their terrible black substance to replace his primitive throwing stick, for which he showed gratitude (but he was not too grateful; superiors do not show much of that feeling to inferiors).

But there was one last ceremony: they escorted him some distance from the camp and then, as one, they all bowed to him and said, 'Good Fortune, warrior of The Great Lord.'

And then they were gone and he was alone again.

He stood for a moment staring in the direction of their village. He had learned much from them but it had all been negative: how to thrust, how to parry, how to deliver the killing stroke. He hoped that those new skills would not be needed in whatever lay ahead of him.

He thrust the Lords of the Sands from his mind and turned away from their direction, seeking to find the hill again. He found it without much difficulty as it was the only elevation of any size in the entire region and immediately set off towards it.

He travelled for many periods of light and darkness; encountered many obstacles, faced and overcame many dangers – none of which shall be recounted here.

And so it was that eventually he came to the foot of the hill that had dominated his thoughts for so long and gazed up at its mysterious summit.

And then he began the arduous climb to the top.

Five

Shana could not quite remember when she had first begun to wonder if there was something wrong with The Universe. It was like trying to recall the crazy events of a dream; trying to hook meaning out of the befuddled illogic of sleep. Try as she might, the reason for that thought would not stay in her grasp but slipped out like a quicksilver fish.

But there *was* such a doubt even if she could not express her reasoning in a chain of syllogisms.

She lay on the soft bank of the river looking up at the bright viridian sky, recently awakened from a light doze. Small puffy clouds moved lazily in that sky as if they knew they had somewhere to go but were in absolutely no hurry to get there. She moved her strong brown arms out behind her and stretched, cat-like, before getting to her feet.

She had somewhere to go but could not quite remember why.

Shading blue-grey eyes from the bright ceiling of iridescent green which comprised the sky she looked around. Things appeared to be as she recalled them: the great shining glaucous band of the river snaked nearby; beyond it she could see the sparkling facets of the crystalline grazing creatures, moving slowly and heavily in the coppery expanses of the varma plants that were their only form of sustenance.

No – no clues here: everything was as it should be.

Her long legs carried her to the riverbank and she looked down at her reflection; as usual somewhat blurred by the whirls and swirls of the currents. Yes – she looked the same; the same smooth, oval face topped with a tumbling mass of amber-gold hair; the same faintly wistful expression as if somewhere she nursed a sad secret.

No – no clues there either.

Why did she feel that she had realised some tremendous truth in her half-sleep as she had lain there on the soothing vegetation and let it escape? Why?

She saw something dart in the water and instinctively she bent down and caught it between her slim fingers, bringing it up into the light.

It was a common glassfish, completely transparent and sparkling in the green light. She held it up to the sky, rejoicing as the cool viridian light streamed through its body, completely uninterrupted by any organs or internal structure.

Although she had seen glassfish many times, she felt puzzled: how could it dart here and there in the shallows when it seemed to be carved out of a single sparkling gemstone? She knew she had an internal structure, she could feel the bone of her skull beneath its coating of flesh; see the tendons move in her wrist when she flexed her hand; feel the hard core in the centre of her breasts on the occasions that she had caressed herself but the glassfish had none of these. How was it that she had not noticed these things before?

She shook her head as if somehow that would clear it and drive these mysterious doubts away. Of course, nothing of the kind happened. She looked around: were there any clues in the landscape?

All looked as it should do; everything was sparklingly clear in the bright skyshine; everything was that rich, riotous medley of greens she loved so much. The skyshine wasn't simply pure green of course, it was merely brightest in the green part of its spectrum. (How did she know that?) Hence, everything looked peaceful and restful in its various multitudes of green - dark green, light green, aquamarine, turquoise, viridian, emerald and many more which only an experienced eye like Shana's could distinguish.

But because there were other colours in the skyshine there

36

were occasional breaks in the otherwise endless carpet of greens. Take that distant ridge of low hills for instance; it was not aquamarine; it was a definite shade of dark blue. Some of the flowers as well, there were colours that could only be described as yellow and red; although the red was very dark due to that colour being the weakest part of the skyshine spectrum.

Shana decided that there was no more she could do to drive this troublesome notion that something was amiss and was about to turn from the river when she heard something moving behind her. She spun around alert and wary. (Why wary? – she had never been concerned about noises around her before.)

She relaxed and smiled – it was only one of the crystalline grazing beasts. It was about hip height and four-legged with a shell-like covering over its back. It was translucent rather than transparent like a glassfish, and there were shadowy shapes within its sparkling carapace that pulsed slowly and rhythmically. As usual it showed no signs of recognising Shana's existence and ploughed steadily on past her, looking for varma plants. It was strange to find one of this side of the river for there were few varma on this bank.

She walked alongside it for a while watching it snuffle around in the ordinary vegetation, looking for varma.

'You're a bit like me, aren't you?' Shana murmured. Her voice was clear and melodious, but not soft – there was steel under the smooth surface of her words, 'lost, looking for something that you're not sure you'll find. Off you go, old friend.'

Completely oblivious to her kind words the grazing creature shuffled off, still searching for the nutritious varma. Shana watched it go, wondering what it was like to be a simple grazing beast; not to concern oneself with thoughts that could not be resolved, questions that could not be answered. There was another thing that she envied in the dull-witted creatures – companionship. Although their numbers waxed and waned with the varma season there were always a fair number of them, trundling along in the coppery fields that held their sustenance.

They did a very odd thing at the start of the varma season; one that Shana had observed many times but still did not understand. At those times, when the first bronze shoots were starting to appear, two of the creatures would approach each other and position their rear ends so that each was touching the other. They would stay in this position for some time with their bodies shaking in a movement that became more and more intense. Then they would move away. Shana had observed that some periods later there would be a number of very small grazers in the herd.

Were the two observations connected in any way? Shana could not see how. How could touching rear ends have anything to do with the appearance of small grazers?

Where could they have come from? Shana was sure nothing like that could be relevant to her own existence. She had no openings that a small Shana could pop out of and in any case there wasn't another Shana that she could touch ends with.

The grazer had disappeared into the green expanses and there were no others to stir her curiosity. But the feeling that it would be nice to have another Shana around lingered. Maybe if there was she could try touching ends to see if anything happened.

Another problem that could not be solved.

She determined to put these strange thoughts behind her – as for this belief that she should be going somewhere: where was there to go? There were only the verdant fields, the lazily winding river, the plains where varma grew abundantly. The world was the world. There was nothing else.

Just a world with nothing in it but a few harmless beasts and one foolish Shana, dreaming of things that could not possibly be.

She wandered back to her little camp by the riverside. It was just a simple affair of logs stacked to form walls with dried varma fronds over the top to act as a shield against the brightest time of the skyshine. There was no door for there was nothing in her world that had ever threatened her, nor did the temperature vary much, even in the time of darkness; no windows, for the scenery never changed except the colour of the varma plains. Her bed was just a pile of the same fronds as made up the roof; simply younger ones which were softer and more pliable.

A small log cut into a cylinder served as a chair and she sat down on it and opened the jar which contained her evening meal. It was another type of fish which swam so lazily in the nearby river that they appeared not to care if they lived or died. They were raw because Shana knew nothing of fire and they were perfectly edible as they were, the only issue being that they were somewhat sweet, which became cloying if one foolishly attempted to eat a great number. There were also a few brownish ovoids which were varma seed pods. These had a pleasant savoury, earthy tang which compensated for the sweetness of the fish. She sat there enjoying her meal, listening to the pleasant gurgling noises from the river and feeling the warmth of the day on her nearly naked skin. Her breasts hung freely but she had a strip of varma fronds around her crotch. She didn't know why she did that as it was never cold in her home by the river but it just felt like the right thing to do.

She finished the last seed pod and wiped the traces of fish from her lips. Although they were crystalline, like nearly all of the living things in her domain, the crystals turned soft and pleasantly chewy when in the mouth. It suddenly occurred to her that she was the only living thing that she knew that was not crystalline. Was there a reason for that?

Of course not. It was just the way things were. She really must stop questioning everything!

She wondered what she should do next. To someone newly arrived in her world life would have seemed distinctly unexciting. There was just the river, the fish, the grazers.

Shana simply found it pleasant and just-right.

With the grace of a large cat, she rose from her simple chair and gave another great stretch. Another walk along the riverbank, she thought to herself.

But as she stepped outside she was aware of a change in the quality of the light. Looking up she saw what she expected to see – at the exact zenith a small black dot had appeared. The time of darkness was upon the Land. As she watched in pleasant contemplation, the dot became an ever-growing circle, swallowing up more and more of the sky until the glowing green was banished to the horizons. And then that thin band of emerald winked out and the Land was in darkness. Total absolute darkness. Vision was completely useless. All she was aware of was the pleasant scents of the Land and the liquid whisperings of the river.

She raised her eyes to where she knew the zenith was, straining to see if there was some structure in that ebon vault – something she had never done before.

There was none.

Despite the total, absolute blackness she felt no concern. This was normality and nothing in her world was any threat, in the time of light or the time of darkness.

And then she saw it: perhaps far away but in reality at some unguessable distance, there shone a light.

A light where no light had ever shone before.

Six

Shana stood watching the light for quite a while, experiencing the sensation of feeling her heart racing for the first time. This really was something new. Normally the time of darkness was the time in which all the Land's creatures, including her, closed their eyes and entered that period of immobility known as sleep. It was the time that her mind appeared to break free of its body and go wandering in unknown lands, free of the bounds of logic. In those times she had seen many strange sights; once she saw a land where the ground had heaved up into mighty peaks which reached into a sky that bore an unusual colour, a colour that she hardly ever saw in her waking times. On another voyage she had seen a black sky, quite like her own sky in the time of darkness but pierced by dimensionless points of light, differing in brightness and hue.

She stood in the warm darkness watching the light. Once or twice it flickered as if some object had passed in front of it but eventually she grew tired of watching, as those events were not repeated. She carefully walked exactly backwards until she encountered her hut. She felt its contours and calculated in her mind in what direction she was looking. Then, finally, she turned, went in and allowed sleep to claim her.

She awoke to find that a thin greenish light had returned to the world. She rushed outside in time to see that the sky was now encircled by a thin band of light. As she watched, the previous day's sequence was repeated in reverse: the horizon-girdling band grew steadily wider with the light becoming stronger as the blackness was banished to an ever-shrinking circle of darkness. Eventually it dwindled to a mathematical point and soundlessly vanished.

Shana had seen that process many times but it always

41

fascinated her. But now she had another phenomenon to investigate.

She positioned herself exactly where she had stood in the previous time of darkness and looked out across the Land. She found herself looking at the exact centre of the range of low hills. So that's where the light had been! She felt her heart beat faster once again as she contemplated the fact that something new and different had occurred in the Land's placid routine.

What to do? she asked herself. Should she just shrug and accept that a light had appeared where there had never been a light before? After all, it was foolish to believe that she had seen all that the Land had to offer. Maybe this kind of thing was perfectly natural but merely infrequent. It was simpler to yawn, stretch, walk down to the river, doze for a while, wake, stretch again and catch a fish – perhaps if she was lucky something a bit more edible than a glassfish.

She stood there for a while in the warm, comforting embrace of the skyshine, irresolute, confused. What to do? What to do?

Then suddenly she knew. She could not spend another time of light repeating the same worn groove of existence. That light must mean something; somehow it was calling her.

She turned and went back into the hut. She had few things she could take; the Land was so warm and gentle she needed no more clothes than the strip she was wearing.

She wrapped a few of the food fish in varma leaves and placed them in a kind of satchel which she flung over one brown shoulder. She took no weapon for there were none in the Land. There was no need for weapons in a world where no creature threatened any other. She strode on, glancing up at the sky to admire the green and gold flying things as they circled high above her.

The hills seemed farther away than she had imagined; they had not appeared to get larger in her vision no matter how long

42

she had been walking and she was forced to stop and rest much more than she had expected. Sweat began to trickle down her hitherto unblemished forehead and get into her eyes. With growing irritation, she wiped it away more and more frequently. It was almost as if the hills were mocking her by their refusal to get any nearer.

Why am I doing this? she said to herself on more than one occasion but for some reason she could not explain or understand she would find herself trudging through the clinging vegetation towards her intended destination.

At last the ground began to slope upwards and the Land's lush greenery began to thin out and become patchy. The soft, fleshy fronds of the usual vegetation were slowly replaced by blackish shrubs which had a twisted, gnarled look about them that she didn't like. As she was passing close to one she suddenly felt a strange and most unwelcome feeling in her thigh. It was nothing like she had ever known before and she went down on one knee with shock. She lay there for some time before venturing to see what had happened to her leg. To her amazement there was a thin red line from one side of the thigh to the other; a line which was slowly oozing a viscous liquid. She looked at the bush she had just passed and was astounded to see that its branches had small, sharp barbs on it, one of which held a drop of the same liquid that was dribbling down her leg!

This was unheard of! There were no such shrubs anywhere else in the Land and this new feeling – what was it? Then unbidden a word came to her from some hitherto unknown region of her mind and that word was *pain*. This was pain.

Pain. A short ugly word. She had never known pain before; until this moment there had only been the comforting warmth, the green glow of the sky, the darting fish on the gentle river. But now there was pain.

Yet somehow the feeling did not deter her. She looked at the hills, now close and rising relentlessly to hide part of the sky, and she felt a new determination to complete this weird journey. They didn't look inviting, for even the thorny bushes became fewer and fewer until they were gone entirely leaving nothing but gravel and rock.

She stood up and immediately realised that the time of darkness was near and glancing up she saw the old familiar disc of blackness growing in the sky, banishing the pleasing green radiance. As usual, she lay down and waited for the warm darkness to enfold her.

And waited.

The darkness came but not the warmth. She soon felt another new and unwelcome sensation and was not too surprised when another new word swam inexplicably into her consciousness and this time the word was *cold*.

She found that *cold* was not too dissimilar to *pain* and that there was no way to escape it. So she lay there on the hard ground, covering herself with some strips from the few thornless nearby plants and waited for sleep to come.

And it did come but not before she saw the light in the hill again; now much larger and brighter.

And as she stared at it she thought to herself: Tomorrow I will find out what you are.

And she slept.

* * *

She became dimly aware that the time of light had returned and tried to rise into a standing position. To her surprise she found that her limbs were reluctant to move and felt stiff and – what was the new word? – yes, *cold*.

Nevertheless, she finally forced reluctant legs into a vertical position and scanned her surroundings. Immediately in the clear light she saw that in a cliff face not too far distant there was a large hole in the rock, an entrance into the inside of the cliff. But

44

an entrance to what?

With new energy she threw away her empty satchel and continued her journey, feeling welcome strength slowly seeping back into her limbs. It occurred to her that if she was to spend any significant time in this new area she would need more covering over her body that had hitherto been necessary.

Finally, she reached the entrance and stood for a moment staring into it. The light did not penetrate far and both the floor and walls of the orifice were unnaturally smooth as if some power had carved them. For a dizzying moment a tumultuous doubt overtook her.

Go back! A portion of her mind called out, *there is pain here!*

She looked back over her shoulder. Below the entrance lay the Land, green and welcoming, an old friend where there had never been either cold or pain. She could see the river, shrunken now to a silvery thread in which at that very moment the glassfish must be darting.

Determination to solve this mystery reclaimed her and she stepped into the dim tunnel.

No sooner had she done so then there was a great rumbling noise behind her and she spun around to see a massive slab of rock slide down, cutting off the green sky and the green landscape.

There was absolute blackness. But only for a moment. Then the walls of the cave suddenly gave off a harsh yellowish light, throwing her surroundings into a mosaic of sulphur and ebony.

She stood completely motionless. It was obvious that this was merely the first event in whatever was planned for her.

She did not have to wait long. A section of the curved wall opened soundlessly and two creatures came out. They were very short, hardly reaching about her knees and, like most things she knew apart from herself, of a crystalline appearance. In the yellow light their bodies were of a smoky, sickly cast, as if pestilence lurked within. They had squarish faces, with lipless

45

mouths stretching from side to side and some distance beyond.

'Oh yes!' the nearer one said as it approached her, 'we have someone to play with at last!' Its voice was high pitched and very shrill in a way that made her wince at first.

Both came up to her and stood either side of her, but very close so that each one could grasp a knee. Their grasp was cold and hard.

'Yes, play with,' the other said in an identical voice, 'Play. We will like that.'

'What – who are you?' Shana finally managed to gasp out. The creatures' appearance did not immediately disturb her but never in her life had she heard beings speak before. It was as if the stones themselves had cried out.

'We are we,' was the mysterious reply from both of the creatures in unison. 'That's all you need to know. Now will you play with us?'

Shana drew back slightly, seeing if they would release the pressure on her knees. They did, but only slowly, reluctantly.

'And what if I don't?'

'Then you will stay here with us forever and ever. And we will find new ways to play with you.'

Shana looked down on the strange pair with growing distaste. Was that a veiled threat? She decided that she must agree to their demands for the time being. Surely they could mean her no harm. Why would harm have suddenly come into her life? There was no harm in the Land below. And then a thought occurred to her. *No harm in the Land. But what if you were a food fish?* She shuddered ever so slightly and then threw the thought off.

'Let's play,' she said.

The creatures looked briefly at each other and then ran around each other, clapping their translucent hands.

'There,' one said to the apparently identical other, 'I told you she would play!'

Shana stared at her new companions and felt an odd

46

sensation as if small things were crawling under her skin. Once again she had learned a new word without thinking about it and this new word was: *Danger*. There had been no danger in the Land – but now there was.

Her mouth was dry when she finally said: 'What do I call you?'

The one to her left said, 'I am Zarka.'

The one standing hungrily to her right said, 'I am Akraz.'

And then they said, 'And you are Shana.'

'How do you know that?'

'Oh, we know you. We have watched you down in the soft green lands.'

Impossible, Shana thought, *it is too far away*. But her sense of unease increased.

Her mouth was even drier now and she had difficulty forming the words but finally she said, 'And what do we play?'

The two looked at her with eyes of pellucid crystal. Crystal that had no discernible depth; that might have been endlessly deep or trivially shallow.

'Name us.'

'That's easy,' Shana began, 'you are ...'

She stopped; the little beings had suddenly begun to race around her in dizzying circles. Then they suddenly stopped and took up what seemed to be their original positions, looking up at her with their unnatural, fathomless eyes.

'Name us.'

Shana felt her heart give a little shudder. She stared at them. Were there any differences?

There were. The one on the left had a mouth that reached slightly farther around its head. But which one?

She had to decide... She pointed to the left hand one and said: 'You are Zarka.'

'Wrong,' the one on the right said. Was there a slight tone of satisfaction in that thin, high-pitched voice? All at once they moved forward and began pinching the soft flesh of her thighs with their hard fingers. She cried out and moved backwards but they followed, pinching, pinching. And then they stopped.

'Every time you get something wrong we will pinch you,' the one with the shorter mouth said.

Shana stood her ground, panting. Once again she was experiencing a new sensation and this time the word was – *Anger*. What right had these creatures to torment her like this? Nothing had ever behaved like this before so why now?

'And if I get the play right will you let me go?'

'Of course.'

'Then let's have the next game.'

'Very well. Here in the hills we are great admirers of logic. Do you know of logic?'

'I know what you mean but I have had little use for it.'

'You will find you need it here.'

Another veiled threat? Shana's mind was torn between anger and alarm.

'Get on with it.'

One of the little creatures moved forward slightly.

'Here in the hills we are of two types: one type always speaks the truth and we call them Truthers. The other type always lies and we call them Liars.'

Shana stared down at what were now clearly revealed to be her captors. What madness was this? Why would any being deliberately lie?

'And so?' she finally demanded.

They once again did their dizzying circling of her and once they had stopped one pointed to the other and said, 'I am a Liar but my companion is a Truther. Now decide what is our reality.'

Their captive stared at them in growing horror. This was not what she was accustomed to; this was not a pleasant nap in the green skyshine or a relaxing walk by the gurgling river.

Think! Think! What could be determined from what the

48

thing had said?

Slowly, thinking as she spoke, she said, 'If you were a Truther then what you said would be true. So, you must be a Liar. But if you are a Liar then all of what you said must be a lie so – so – '... The answer was there, she knew it! Just think carefully!

She had it!

'So, all of what you said must be a lie. So, your companion is a Liar also!'

Her statement ended on a rising note of triumph. She had it!

Silence fell. The creatures did not move and simply stared at her.

Then one spoke.

'That is correct. You may go.'

There was no emotion in the voice. No disappointment, simply a statement of fact.

They turned and the wall swung open to receive them.

She was alone.

Seven

She stood there in the tunnel and found herself shivering. Partly it was the cold but partly it was not. She had just had a profound shock and her mind was still whirling from the implications of her current situation; all of them unpleasant it seemed.

She had to get out of this place! She turned back to the slab of rock that had barred the entrance to this world and scrabbled vainly at it, breaking her soft, shaped nails in the process. Useless. She could not possibly even scratch it. She was trapped.

For a brief moment tears misted her eyes. Why had she come? Why had she not stayed in the safe and sheltering womb of the Land? There had been this strange compulsion to explore but where had that come from?

Abruptly there was no more time to ponder. She realised that where she stood, next to the unyielding mass of stone, the light was fading. And yet at the other end of the cave or tunnel, whatever it was, the light was growing stronger. Clearly, she was being directed further into the bowels of the hills, deeper into its maw.

There was nothing more she could do here; she would have to follow the unspoken command and move further in, to whatever was now planned for her.

She walked for some time, followed by a creeping mass of darkness as if being stalked by a horrific black beast. Her surroundings never changed significantly from the dispiriting melange of black and yellow.

And then she came to the end of the tunnel and was faced by a great wall of impenetrable grey stone. She stared at it in despair. Was this to be her end – to starve to death in the guts of these awful hills? She stood and stared at the wall as if willing it to dissolve and evaporate. And then she noticed that near the bottom of this wall there was the faint but unmistakable outline of a door.

She approached, somehow fearfully and hopefully simultaneously. If there was a door there must be something beyond it – was that not logic? She ran her torn fingers over the rough surface until she found that there was a small protrusion on it; one she could get a grip on.

She pulled it and although made of rock the door opened easily, soundlessly, smoothly. She stepped through.

Disappointment hit her at once – it was just the same as the other side. Bare rock, lit by a foetid, sulphurous light. No hope.

She stood there motionless, overcome by the hopelessness of her situation. Time passed. How long? It was impossible to say in an environment where nothing changed.

And then she detected a movement right at the limit of her peripheral vision. She spun around, startled and repulsed by the form that now stood before her.

It was very similar to the unpleasant twins that she had recently encountered with the same hard, translucent form, the same lipless mouth transversing most of the head. But it was taller, its head level with her bosom.

'What – who are you?' she demanded.

'You know me,' was the sibilant, high-pitched reply, 'I am Zarka.'

She stared at the thing in stunned silence for a moment. Then: 'Impossible. It was smaller than you. I have just left it. You are not Zarka.'

The thing moved toward her. She stood her ground.

'Nevertheless, I am Zarka. Your beliefs are of no concern to me, only your abilities. Your strengths, your weaknesses. I must know if you are fit to be a warrior.'

Shana somehow knew what the ugly word meant although she had never encountered it before.

'I am not a warrior. I just want to go back to the Land.'

'There are two ways to leave this place. Neither involves you returning to the Land. That degenerate existence is over.'

Shana found that something was replacing the fear that had turned her limbs to mush. A determination to outface this creature.

'What do you want?'

It moved closer still.

'To play some games.'

Not this again! Shana groaned inwardly. She looked down into the repulsive eyes.

'Get on with it.'

'Of course.' And then it hit her.

She tumbled backwards and hit the floor of the cavern, hard. Lights danced in front of her, pain coursed through her jaw where she had been hit. Her teeth felt suddenly loose.

She spat out blood and glared up at her tormentor.

'What game is this?'

'The most basic game of all – the game of struggle, the game to see who has supremacy.'

'There is no reason to fight. No need to see who is supreme. Why should we not co-operate for the common good?'

No answer.

'I don't wish to play.'

'If you do not play then I will know immediately that you are not worthy. Then I will kill you.'

She stood up, knowing that to back away, to run, to beg for mercy – all would be futile. She would have to play.

And play she did. She rushed at the creature and then, turning slightly, shot out a long leg so that her foot struck its chest, dead centre. It staggered, went down on one knee but did not fall.

'Excellent,' it said. 'Exc...'

It did not finish the sentence as Shana, copying its earlier attack, brought her fist up under the point of the jaw, putting all

52

of her not inconsiderable strength behind it. The substance of the creature, although crystalline in appearance, was more rubbery in texture and resilience. Already on one knee it crashed to the ground and lay there on its back.

'That was good,' it said, 'you have some strength after all.'

But then it leapt to its feet. 'But how much?'

Then it was moving all around her in a whirl of stabbing blows, blows that she did not see coming and could not defend against. Eventually she collapsed into black unconsciousness.

She awoke with the metallic sting of blood in her mouth. One eye was closed.

Roughly she was pulled to her feet and held so that her assailant's face was almost against her breasts.

'You have failed the test. But let's try another. You are better at logic than physical effort it would appear.'

It dragged her across the floor to where stood three boxes. All were made of stone but of different colours: black, white and red.

It left her lying in front of the boxes and showed her what it held in one hand. The object had a short black handle from which protruded a gleaming blade of a substance that Shana did not recognise.

As if reading her thoughts, the creature (Zarka?) said, 'This substance is what we call steel. It is fashioned into a blade. A very sharp blade.'

Shana knew what a blade was. Some of the plants in the Land had leaves that looked like that blade. But they were not made of steel.

It continued, 'I have put another of these objects – which we term "dagger" by the way – in one of these boxes. Now read what is written on the boxes.'

Shana had never seen writing before but somehow she knew that she would be able to read whatever the inscriptions were. And she could. With her one good eye she saw on the black box:

"The dagger is in this box". On the white box she read: "The dagger is not in this box". On the red box she read "The dagger is not in the black box."

She knew her captor was behind her and heard it say: 'At most one of these statements is true. Where is the dagger?'

Shana stared down at the boxes. But this time there was no despair. The solution came into her mind almost instantly.

She turned and stared down at that inhuman visage. 'The problem is trivial. The black box statement and the red box statement are the opposite of each other. One must be true. As at most one of these statements is true then the statement on the white box is false. The dagger is in the white box.'

She whirled and flung up the lid of the white box. There lay the dagger which she snatched out and pointed at her inquisitor.

As usual, no emotion was shown.

'As you demonstrated, you have solved this problem.'

'And I will solve the next problem,' the panting woman rasped, 'maybe I will solve it with this dagger!'

'That is good,' the being replied, unmoved, 'the desire for revenge, to kill – these are admirable motives.'

And with that, it turned away. A section of wall opened before it. It passed in and once again she was alone.

* * *

She awoke, realising that her tormented body had demanded rest. As before she felt cold and stiff and once again she saw that the light was changing in her prison, as before forcing her to retreat further into the hill.

She pondered her situation for a while. Should she just accept that it was hopeless and that she should just lay down and die?

No, she decided, perhaps there would be an end to these sadistic problems and she would win through to freedom. There was only one way to find out.

She accepted the gradual, intangible pressure of the changing light and moved away from the approaching darkness. Once again she found herself walking down a yellow-lit tunnel but this time with aching limbs and the memory of pain.

She came to a door; identical to the one she had passed through earlier. She hesitated for a short while, knowing that some kind of ordeal undoubtedly awaited her on the other side. But then she pulled it open and stepped through.

She was in a room, apparently unoccupied. She groaned aloud when she saw that on one side were two stone boxes, white and red. Another mind-twisting problem awaited her it seemed. But then she saw something new. There was a shelf jutting out from the wall and in the ochre and black shadows some objects were reflecting the lurid illumination of the room.

She picked up one of the three objects that were lying on the shelf. It was like the dagger that the Zarka-thing had shown her but much bigger with a long, straight blade. She carefully touched an edge. It was wickedly sharp. But what was it?

'We call it a sword,' came a hissing, high-pitched voice from behind her. 'They are part of my personal collection of beloved treasures.'

Fleshless fingers tore the sword from her grasp and pulled her into the centre of the room. And there before her was another of the eldritch denizens of this subterranean purgatory. But once again it was similar but different. It had the same quasi-crystalline appearance, the same lipless gash of a mouth, the same weird, pellucid eyes which possessed that penetrating gaze. But it was taller, much taller.

Shana was tall but this thing stood a head taller than her. For the first time she had to look up to meet a disturbing stare.

'And who are you?' she eventually said, 'Zarka again I suppose.'

'No,' came the languid reply, 'I am Akraz, obviously.'

'Obviously,' Shana said, 'And what meaningless tests do you have for me this time?'

'Our tests are not meaningless. They are designed to see whether or not you possess the physical and mental qualities necessary to become a warrior. At present the results are inconclusive.'

'A warrior. That implies an army, I believe.' (Shana had no idea how she knew all this but know it she did.) 'And in whose army would I be a warrior?'

'Why the Lord Korok's of course. Who else has the power to command an army?'

Korok. A flat, ugly word. It had no music, no gentleness. It was a word that would not be spoken in the Land below.

'And who is Lord Korok?'

'My master. Your master. He is everyone's master.'

'I understand,' Shana continued, not understanding at all, 'And now Akraz, or whatever you are, given your lust for violence I suppose we fight. With those swords you love so much perhaps?'

'No, those tests are complete and you will never pollute my treasures with your touch again. You have shown some physical ability, surprising in one so flimsily constructed. You have also shown a certain degree of reasoning power, although the tests are, as you yourself said, elementary.

'There is one final mental test for you. On the result of this will be decided if you are fit to be a warrior of the great lord. And therefore, of the greater lord whom he serves.'

'But of course,' Shana said, 'what more could I possibly expect or want?'

Irony was clearly lost on Akraz and it turned and pointed to the boxes.

'I have put a precious object in one of these boxes; now read the inscriptions.'

Shana obeyed, once again not knowing how it was possible

for her to do so.

The first white box had on its lid the somewhat disturbing words: "This box does not contain the fatal scimitar."

The second had the message: "Exactly one of these two statements is true."

Shana stood over them, wracked with indecision. This was a different type of problem; she could see that. It all depended on the interpretation she gave to the inscription on the red box. Rapidly she considered the case where that statement was true and the implication of that, and then the opposite and the implication of that.

Eventually it was clear to her.

She pointed to the white box. 'There.'

'Open it.'

She opened it.

It was empty.

Akraz came up behind her. 'You have failed to understand the concept of self-reference and that these statements lead to a contradiction given that the scimitar was in the red box. Therefore, you have failed the entire set of tests. You are not a warrior.'

Shana stood motionless. What had gone wrong? She had been certain of her powers of reasoning. She slumped, feeling the tone drain from her muscles, feeling her drive to fight on evaporate.

'What now?' she muttered thickly, already knowing the answer.

'The Lord Korok has no use for those who are not warriors. If you are not a warrior then you must be a Degenerate.'

Shana turned around to stare up at this fiendish entity. 'And what happens to Degenerates?'

'Eventually they are killed. We will move immediately to that outcome.'

Akraz opened the red box and took something out. It was

57

made of metal, long curved metal.

It gleamed obscenely in the sulphurous light.

'The fatal scimitar,' Akraz commented dispassionately, 'its purpose is obvious.'

Shana backed away from the terrible thing. This was the apotheosis; the supreme moment. In the next few seconds hung her continued existence; her life; her death.

What could be done? Akraz stood motionless before her. In the next few seconds it would lift the fatal scimitar and bring it down upon her. It could not be directly attacked – it was too big for that and the scimitar would slash through her as she tried to leap upon its wielder.

But a surge of furious, magmatic anger swept through her arteries. No! She would not die today in this foul place at the hands of this foul thing!

In the depths of her mind she saw the one course of action she could take and instantly she took it.

She flung herself on the floor, rolling like a wounded animal, crying, begging, pleading: 'No don't do it! Please don't kill me!'

Akraz grunted. 'The way of the Degenerate.' It did not move and there seemed to be a flicker of animation in its otherwise toneless voice. It lowered the scimitar so its view of the writhing supplicant was unobstructed. The wicked point of the weapon drew a fine white line on the unyielding stone of the floor. 'This is the meaning of your disgusting lives – to prepare for this consummation.'

Shana continued to grovel and squirm on the floor. Over she rolled, occasionally looking at her executioner with her one good eye, all the time getting imperceptibly closer to her goal.

Then Akraz saw the danger. It stiffened, raised the scimitar and lunged forward.

Too late. With one lightning leap Shana stood upright, turned, picked up the nearest sword, whirled back with the weapon in her hands. Two-handed she wielded it and in a blur of savage steel, the sword followed a dreadful arc, driven by all the strength the woman owned. That arc of death reached Akraz's neck and, unimpeded, continued its path. The creature's head left its body and bounced once on the floor. There was no blood.

Shana crashed back against the shelf which now only held two swords. She began to tremble violently and broke out into great, gasping sobs as if rising from near-drowning.

It was over. It was over.

And then she felt something on her ankle. Looking down she saw that the headless trunk had dragged itself across the floor and a hand was touching her leg, trying to grasp it. Beyond, Akraz's head had stopped its rolling so that the face was looking directly at her. One of the eyes blinked.

She pulled herself away from the questing fingers and instinctively she raised the terrible sword and thrust it down on the thing's torso where the heart should have been. It passed straight through and recoiled slightly as it hit the floor.

The body shuddered and then was still. The eyes on the head closed. And then slowly, slowly both ghastly things began to change. They softened, blurred, ran together as both head and body gently subsided into separate pools of glutinous slime. The slime bubbled slightly and then, abruptly, became solid and opaque.

All was still.

Shana stepped around the now motionless pools, careful not to get too near to them.

She stood at the opposite end of the room from where she had entered, occasionally casting nervous glances over her shoulder.

Nothing. No door. She was trapped with the obscene remnants of her captor. A lingering death awaited.

And then before her astounded eyes the faint outline of a door began to appear in the solid stone. It grew more clearly delimited until it was obviously a real door. And then it opened.

She gazed at the ineffable marvel of the sky; the lovely, beautiful sky framed in the doorway. But why had the door appeared and opened? Was there some higher power that had been watching both her and Akraz?

She stepped out onto a wide ledge, feeling a cool breeze drift over her bruised, semi-naked form.

Below her stretched an unknown territory; a territory that was not her beloved Land, for it had none of that domain's verdant lushness.

It was dotted with low trees and bushes, both of a dull, uninspiring glaucous shade.

But beyond, nearly on the horizon, stood a strange hill. It was oddly regular, with a flat top. And from that summit rose a blueish column that might have been smoke but was not.

Shana stared at it for some time, forgetting to look behind her, back into the dreadful room.

There was something about that hill that entranced her. It was as if it had some strange magnetic pull upon her.

Surely this is what had called her up into the horrific hills she had just exited. Surely here were the answers that she so desperately craved.

She glanced back into the cave of horrors where she could just make out the congealed pools of filth on the floor.

With narrowed eyes she snarled: 'Farewell monsters. It was your misfortune to meet with a warrior today.'

There was no longer any need for her to debate her choices or to glory in her triumph. Firmly grasping her new sword, she began to descend to the arid plain and begin the long trek to that mysterious hill.

She met many dangers on the way to her destination and overcame them all.

And so it was, at last, she reached the base of the hill and began the arduous climb to the top.

Part Two

One

The climb was arduous but Jon achieved it, although not without some stops to catch his breath on the way. The slope was covered with thorn-studded bushes that were hard to avoid and he had gained a criss-cross pattern of welts by the time he reached his goal.

He finally emerged onto a wide terrace which seemingly encircled the hill about two- thirds of the way up. And that hill was crowded with what could only be dwellings.

And all around were what could only be those that dwelled in them.

People.

Like him.

Jons.

They saw him almost immediately as he came over the lip of the terrace and a crowd came toward him, smiling and gesticulating to him to come further out from the encircling bushes.

Warily he obeyed. He was still not entirely comfortable with the idea that there were actually things in this world that did not want to harm him. But as they came nearer he could see that they were smiling and that there was laughter in their eyes.

'Welcome! Welcome,' the nearest called out as he came up to Jon. He held out a large hand. Jon stared at it for a few seconds before he realised that this must be some kind of greeting. He slowly extended his own which was eagerly seized by the other in a grasp that felt like it could crush rocks. Jon stared at the man as he continued to pump their hands. This person was like him but subtly different. Jon knew roughly what his appearance was from the occasions when he had encountered pools of still water and had assumed that if there were other beings here that they would look just like him.

In a way they did. Jon could see that they all had the basic plan of two legs, two arms, a torso to bear those limbs and a head on top of the torso. But now he was close up to one he could see that the person was not his twin. For a start, he was shorter but at the same time wider. His hair was curlier than Jon's and jet black and Jon was shocked to see that these black curls extended over the man's chest. Jon had assumed that only kabarras were hairy all over.

The man was speaking, speaking in an excited voice.

'Welcome, welcome! It's good to have another here to strengthen our numbers.'

Jon stared at the man. He had no experience of social intercourse and the only beings he had encountered before capable of speech had been the Lords of the Sands who had not given him such a friendly welcome. In fact, the entire concept of peaceful meetings was somewhat alien to him.

Eventually, he understood that some kind of response was expected of him. Looking the man directly in the eye he said slowly, 'I am glad to be here. I am Jon.'

The man nodded as if already knew that. 'Yes Jon21. Welcome. I am Jarz12.'

He turned to the others, who had stopped a little way back in deference to his apparently superior status. 'People! Jon21 has joined us!'

Jon assumed that there had been some kind of misunderstanding.

'No, I said "Jon". My name is Jon.'

The other turned to face him again, still smiling. 'Yes, Jon21. You don't understand how everything works here yet obviously, after all you've only just arrived. But there's plenty of time before we have to go up to the Gate of Light.'

The reverential way that Jarz had uttered that phrase made Jon think he could see the capital letters. "The Gate of Light".

He obviously did have a lot to learn.

Jarz slapped him on the shoulder. 'Come my friend, you've had a long journey I have no doubt. You must be famished. Come with me – there's plenty to eat here.'

The crowd parted to let Jarz and Jon through, all of them smiling as if the most wonderful thing in the world had just happened. All of them were similar in appearance to Jarz and Jon; similar but by no means identical.

Jon looked around at this busy township. He had gone from being the only human in existence to one of many. It was a difficult situation to immediately grasp and he felt more than a little dizzy. And then instead of looking around, he looked up. The flat summit of his new home was not far above and he could now clearly see that enigmatic column of blue *something* jetting up from its centre. It was still impossible to determine what it was a column *of;* now it was so close it shone brilliantly, outlined against the crimson of the sky. It was slightly different each time it was observed from a different angle – sometimes softly lambent, sometimes actinic and harsh. It reached so far up into the sky that the column shrank into a cone before finally disappearing as a mathematical point at some unguessable altitude.

Jarz tapped him gently on the shoulder. 'Come on my friend. You'll have plenty of time to look around!'

Jon and his new companion came up to the nearest building. It was well built, far better than the huts of the Lords of the Sands with strong pillars of polished, richly glowing wood and roofs of gleaming black tiles. Jon ran his hand over one of the pillars: it was silky smooth beneath his fingers and giving off an encouraging warmth.

Jarz saw his pleasure and wonder and grinned good-naturedly. 'Like it? It's yours.'

Jon turned in surprise. 'Mine? But...'

'No buts,' Jarz replied, showing strong, wide teeth, 'we all have our own homes here. Let's go in.'

They did so and Jon looked around, feeling that his capacity for surprise and wonder was being severely stretched. The cool interior was hung with various types of tapestries and there was a window allowing comforting red light in on his otherwise dim surroundings, and, wonder of wonders, there were things that Jarz named as "bed", "chairs" and "table". Jarz invited him to sit on the "chair" and bring it up to the "table."

Sitting on the other side of that structure, Jarz indicated the bowl in its centre.

'It has a selection of cold meats, picked especially for you. Try. Enjoy.'

Jon picked up one the brownish, vaguely rectangular objects in the bowl, sniffed it warily, broke off a piece and slowly put int in his mouth and began chewing, ready to instantly eject it if there was anything slightly suspicious.

He stopped chewing after only a few seconds and stared at his grinning companion.

'It's marvellous! I've never tasted anything like it!'

'Carry on.'

Jon did not really need the encouragement. Whatever it was, it was many times superior to the bland, chewy kabarra meat. It had a dozen flavours all at once and a texture that was neither stickily soft nor impenetrably hard.

'Don't eat it all at once,' Jarz warned him as Jon extended a hand for the next piece, 'It's very rich. You're not used to it. Take another look around.'

Reluctantly, Jon stood up and continued his examination of his new lodgings. Then he stopped rigid. On the other side of the room was another man, a tall, powerful man he had not heard enter. He tensed and drew his short black sword.

'Jon, Jon,' came Jarz's voice behind him, 'you really must learn to trust us. There's no danger here. Go nearer.'

Carefully Jon obeyed, watching the other seemingly doing the same.

Then he realised. It was him! It was his reflection!

He went up to what was now revealed to be a tall mirror of exquisitely polished silvery metal. He put his hand on his reflection's hand in amazement. He had seen himself reflected in water a few times of course but never like this! It was so clear, so still, so real! It was just as if another identical Jon was there, touching his hand. The other stared back at him, a tall figure with brown skin stretched tightly over wide shoulders and ridged abdominal muscles.

And then the other smiled and all was well.

Jon turned around to face Jarz, meeting Jarz's smile with his own.

'This is a world of wonders! I see now why I wanted to come here!'

It was then he noticed something in the corner of the room., in a small alcove. It was a table and chair, somewhat smaller than their dining equivalents. On the table was an object the like of which he had never seen. It was a piece of curved substance which at both ends held flat discs which on one side where covered in soft padding. He picked it up. It had the right dimensions to fit around a person's head.

He turned to his companion, holding the unknown object.

'What is this?'

He was surprised to see Jarz was no longer smiling and instead looked somewhat tense.

'Ah, please put that down Jon.'

'Why? What is it?'

Jarz came up to him and very gently extricated the thing from Jon's fingers.

'We can't tell you everything in one go now, can we? This has a very special purpose which you're not ready for.' He attempted a smile but it was not like his earlier ones. 'You want to keep some surprises for later, surely?'

Jon noted a slight undercurrent to the man's words but was

66

unable to define it. He shrugged. This was no time to pick a quarrel with his new companions. He nodded and put the object back where he had found it.

'Sure. You're right - I don't want all my surprises at once.'

'Let's go back out, 'Jarz suggested, slightly too eagerly. 'There's lots more to see.'

They emerged into the coppery light of late afternoon and continued their tour of the village. The houses had a few variations in design and style but most were of equal quality to Jon's new residence. Everyone looked pleased to see him but as Jon walked he gradually became aware of something he hadn't noticed in the initial excitement of his arrival.

There was marked similarity in appearance in the residents. Apparently there were only four or five basic types. They passed one powerfully built man with coal-black skin and short curly hair. A few minutes later after passing a variety of other people they encountered what appeared to be the same man.

After the second man had safely disappeared into the throng Jon turned to Jarz and said 'How did he get in front of us so quickly? I didn't see him go past.'

Jarz's old relaxed grin was back. 'That was Jern 23 and Jern 16. They're both very square fellows. You'll like them when you get to know them.'

Jon was not quite sure what "square fellows" meant but it sounded approving. It also seemed to fit with the lack of diversity that he had begun to notice. But why would there be different versions of the same person?

Were there different versions of him?

And then suddenly they came to a wicker-type fence that ran from the side of the hill to the lip of the terrace. Beyond the fence, the same type of houses stretched into the distance and around the flank of the hill. There were no people in the immediate vicinity but Jon could see some things moving just as the side of the hill curved away into invisibility.

67

There was something odd about those people – for people they appeared to be. They were noticeably shorter than the people on Jon's side and their physiques appeared to be made of curves rather than straight lines. It was hard to tell; they were so far away.

'Who are those people?' he said, turning to the seemingly all-knowing Jarz.

'That's the village of the women. We don't normally have much to do with them.'

'Why? Are they violent?'

'No, the opposite in fact. They're usually quite friendly. But we don't have much in common and the Lord Korok prefers us not to fraternise.'

An electric thrill passed through Jon's spine.

Korok.

That name again. The name that had saved his life.

'Who is Lord Korok?' he said, speaking very slowly and distinctly.

It appeared that he had not spoken distinctly enough because Jarz totally ignored the question and continued to look around with a vacuous smile on his face.

'Come,' he said, reaching up to slap Jon's shoulder, 'There's nothing for us here. Let's go back.'

They walked back along the dusty track that separated the buildings from the lip of the terrace. Jon remained silent for a while, not sure whether some topics were off-limits or not. Twice now Jarz had reacted in an unexpected way. It was too soon to be concerned, he told himself. This was a new environment and it was not his place to pronounce on what could or could not be discussed. He reminded himself of the near termination he had so narrowly escaped at the hands of the Lords of the Sands and despite the warmth of his surroundings could not prevent a very small shudder.

However, he felt the silence must be broken.

'So what do you all you people do here,' he finally asked, 'there seem to be quite a few of you here. Where do you hunt?'

Jarz gave a small chuckle; the chuckle of the sophisticate for the naïve wonderings of the rural innocent.

'Hunt? We don't hunt! For food at least. The Lord Korok provides for us all. All blessings come from our Lord.'

Jon felt annoyed. All conversations here seemed eventually to terminate in a reference to this "Korok" person - a person who it was apparently forbidden to discuss.

They were getting near Jon's new home and Jon felt more and more irritated by these oblique references to the explanations of the situation he now found himself in. But at that moment he noticed that the light had changed and looking up he was just in time to see the first purple bar appear in the sky.

Ah! Some things still made sense here! he thought to himself. At least the sky was normal.

They halted at the entrance to his dwelling.

'Well I'll leave you here,' Jarz said, his omnipresent smile gleaming in the gathering twilight, 'you must be absolutely exhausted by all that's happened after your long journey. I'll leave you now and we'll talk more in the morning. Enjoy your rest – you've earned it!'

And with that, he turned and moved off into the gathering amaranthine shadows.

Jon watched him go. He stood there until Jarz had disappeared and he was alone. The purple bars multiplied in the sky as he stood there and soon the time of darkness would descend like an enveloping cloak. He turned and went into his house, the interior of which was now bathed in a gentle, comforting pink glow.

As he sat he went over a few things in an oddly troubled mind. He should be satisfied, content, happy even – but he was not.

Once again he had that feeling that there was something

wrong with this paradise, something that didn't make sense.

He decided that perhaps all would be clear in the next time of light.

He went to the bed and lay down. After a period of tossing back and forth, he got up and lay down on the floor.

He slept.

Two

Jon gradually became aware of a soft pinkish glow through his window that could only mean that the new time of light had arrived.

He got up from the floor, still wondering how soft it had felt after the harsh, stony ground that he had been used to until recently. He crossed to his table and was only a little surprised to see that on it there was a pitcher, a tumbler, a bowl and a small object which had a little shallow indentation at one end. His surprise returned however when he picked up the tumbler and realised he could see his fingers grasping it on the other side!

Shaking his head in wonderment he pulled up the chair, which he had now completely mastered, and pulled the bowl towards him. It was filled with a soft white substance from which small tendrils of diaphanous vapour were slowly rising. Whilst wondering how he could pick up such an odd substance he had another epiphany and eagerly seized the implement with the shallow indentation at one end and began to eat his breakfast.

He poured himself some of the liquid from the pitcher into the transparent tumbler and noted that although the room was warm the water was cold. He shrugged: it was time to start accepting rather than wondering.

On another chair near the door he noted a small pile of what appeared to be fabric, which on examination was revealed to be a closefitting tunic, which when worn would cover most of his form, leaving only his head, shoulders and limbs uncovered. He suddenly realised that the scrap of soiled and torn fabric that rather desperately clung to his crotch was no longer suitable for his new surroundings. He glanced down at his torso and ran a finger along one of the white scar lines crossing his brown chest. He thrust the memory away and changed into his new apparel.

He emerged into bright skyshine and was immediately greeted like an old friend by the many passers-by. Some even came up to him to enquire on his general wellbeing. He nodded, forcing underdeveloped facial muscles into smiles, and moved on. He found this endless overt display of emotion alien and slightly uncomfortable after so much time either alone or fighting for his life.

He decided to walk to the wicker fence and try to get a better look at this tribe of Jons that Jarz had identified as "women". There was something about the distant view of them that he had had the previous period that had left him strangely unsatisfied, as if here was yet another mystery that he must resolve. But he had not gone very far when as he attempted to pass a large table seated around which was a crowd of laughing men he was called over to join them. Jon felt that he had no alternative but to join the throng, although he was much more used to his own company. But, he reasoned, if this was to be his new home he must learn to become part of the community; after all everyone else seemed to be enjoying it.

He squeezed himself between the two men who happened to be nearest and a round of introductions began while a pitcher of a liquid that was not water was passed to him.

He sipped it and though, like the water, it was cold it generated a feeling of warmth in his stomach. He liked it.

The one who had called him over was Jal10 and he rapidly introduced the others, who nodded to Jon as their names were announced.

'How are you finding it here?' Jal asked, with another of those gleaming smiles which seemed to be the trademark of this place.

Jon was momentarily lost for words. How was he finding it here?

For quite some time now nothing had tried to kill him or even injure him. Food had mysteriously appeared even when he

72

had not been particularly hungry and without him having to crawl on his belly through undergrowth. It couldn't have been much stranger if he had found himself living at the bottom of one of the forest's lakes.

The others appeared to be waiting for him to give some mark of approval, of approbation.

Words did not come. He did not have the vocabulary. Finally, he found himself uttering a word he had never used before.

'It's very nice,' he said, to no-one in particular.

Did the smiles falter, ever so slightly? He could not be sure.

Jal looked around at his fellow diners and then nodded. 'Of course. It was silly of me to put you on the spot. After all this is all very new to you. Please forgive me.'

An odd silence fell. Finally, Jal asked, 'As you are so new – is there anything you'd like to know? Anything you'd like to ask?'

Jon considered asking if Jal knew anything about the women-people but decided that he would find that out for himself. But there was something to ask, he realised.

'We all have numbers here. Is that because there – there are more than one of us?'

The group gave a noise which Jon hadn't heard before but somehow knew was a "chuckle." Jal tried to keep a straight face and, after almost succeeding, said 'Yes. Of course. Why else would we have numbers?'

Jon was annoyed. Somehow he had given the impression that he was stupid, a rustic nobody. He didn't like that. His sword arm jerked but nobody noticed.

'More than one,' he intoned slowly, 'Jarz called me – uhh – Jon21, I think. Then that means that there are twenty more of me. Where are they?'

Jal leaned across the table and touched Jon's arm. He withdrew it.

'Well Jon,' Jal said carefully, as if explaining something to a

73

small, confused child, 'there are others of you but the Jon-type is particularly prone to mishap. Not that many have managed to get here.'

'So many of the- uhh – Jon-type didn't reach this hill.'

'Yes. You understand.' Jal looked relieved and began to turn to his companion to start a new conversation.

But Jon was not finished. 'If they never got here how did you know their numbers? How do you know I am the twenty-first?'

Jal shrugged. 'We just do. That's all. Have you finished?' His tone had turned cold and neither he nor the others were smiling.

Jon stood up and looked down the table at his erstwhile companions. 'Yes I have. Thank you for the drink'

But Jal had already turned and was busy talking.

Jon walked on.

After some time he stopped and, turning, looked down over the edge of the terrace, back over the terrain he had passed through to get here. Why had he come? Why had he left the forest that he knew and understood? Why had he battled with the Lords of the Sands? His gaze strove to penetrate the distances to their realm but it was lost in the greyish haze on the horizon. It all seemed so long ago now! And for what had he fought – to sit here in the skyshine and eat and drink and indulge in conversations that twisted and turned but got nowhere?

He shook his head. This was not the answer to the tremendous mystery that had drawn him inexorably from the sheltering trees.

This was – nothing.

He walked on for a while longer, hardly lifting his gaze from the ground. Thus it was he suddenly bumped up against the wicker fence and looked up with a cry of surprise.

As usual, there was no one nearby, just vague shapes in the distance. His eyes narrowed. There was certainly something different about them – but what?

74

For some reason he didn't understand, he waved at the distant figure but it didn't respond and, feeling foolish, he let his arm drop and finding himself under a strange dejection began the walk back.

He ignored the cries of greetings and attempts to draw him into conversations as he trudged homeward. He came into his house and sat down heavily in the main chair. His thoughts hung heavy on him as he ran through all that had happened since that peculiar day when he had first felt the stirrings of the great doubt, the doubt that all was well with the world, with his mode of existence. Then he stiffened and his head rose from his chest.

Something wrong. Something missing.

He stood up abruptly and then he realised – his sword, the one given him by the Lords of the Sands – it was gone!

He rushed around the room, overturning the chairs and the table and angrily looking under them. Nothing.

A volcanic anger powered through him. Never in his life had he been without a weapon, never been defenceless! He made a movement to burst out of the house but stopped. Jarz stood in the doorway.

'My, you look upset Jon. Is something wrong?'

Jon strode up to him and stood as close as he could without touching.

'My sword. Where is it?'

'Your sword? That old thing? Why would you want that?'

'I don't need to explain anything to you,' Jon snapped, 'My sword. Where is it?'

Jarz beckoned back into the house. 'Come on. Let's discuss this like grown men. Could you put the chairs back please.'

Jon glared at him for a few moments but decided to not take any precipitate action.

The two went back in and sat down facing each other.

'Jon,' began Jarz, putting his hand out to touch Jon's thigh but apparently then thinking better of it, 'you have to realise we're not going to change to fit in with your old ways. Those were bad days and they're gone. You have to accept that. Our ways are different here and they're better ways. You'll come to realise that.'

'My sword,' Jon growled.

'Is in a safe place. But you really don't need it here. Who are you going to fight? Me? Jon11? Don't be silly.'

While not showing any emotion Jon noted that term. Jon11. So there was another Jon in this place. He tried reason.

'Why didn't you ask me instead of taking it?'

Jarz nodded. 'You're right of course. We should have. It's just that we don't like those things hanging around, except when they're needed.'

Jon's eyes narrowed. Another oblique reference wrapped in ambiguity.

'So there is a way I'll get my sword back?'

Jarz expression became strangely evasive and for a moment he looked away.

'Well, yes, there is a way, usually quite an enjoyable way. But I hope it doesn't come to that until you're ready and you are not the one who's selected. You'll be fine as long as you don't do anything to earn the Lord Korok's disapproval.'

Jon leapt to his feet and stared down at the other.

'Korok! Korok! I'm tired of that name! Who is Korok!'

Jarz stood up slowly and took several steps backwards.

'Jon I will forgive you for that. You're still very inexperienced. But let me give you this warning – this sort of behaviour is not the kind that will endear you to the Lord Korok.'

And with that, he was gone.

Jon stared after him, his fists clenching and unclenching for some time. Then accepting the futility of his actions he sat down on the small chair in the alcove and picked up the curved object he had noticed earlier. He turned it over and over and over in his large hands trying to determine its purpose.

It was no good – he could not. In yet another burst of exasperation he flung it away and stood up and, for want of anything more productive to do, strode back and forth.

On one of his strides in the direction of the door he noticed a small piece of material in the doorway that had not been there before. He picked it up and flattened it out, expecting to see words on one side.

He was not disappointed.

And this is what he read: "I am with you. You are right. Things are not what they seem. I will be in touch. Jon11."

He rushed to the door. The path outside his house was empty.

Three

Nothing else happened in the remainder of the evening and Jon was finally forced to accept that no mysteries were to be resolved that day. When the time of darkness came, he tried sleeping in the bed-thing. It was horribly soft, like slowly sinking into a warm swamp and eventually Jon gave it up in favour of the floor, although he had stayed in it longer than on his first attempt. Dreams came to him that dark time; dreams of his past experiences, images of hunting kabarras in the undergrowth with shafts of crimson light beaming through the great canopy in intangible columns. Once again he fought the champions of the Lords of the Sands and once again came near to oblivion.

The day passed.

Then another.

Times of darkness and times of light succeeded each other with metronomic precision.

Then on one morning, after another light-period round of fruitless and futile questioning and after yet another perfectly timed breakfast, he stood for a while wondering how to fill yet another quotidian day. He stood before the mirror and stared at his body where already he thought he could detect a slight slumping in his forest-toned musculature, a gradual softening, a slow blurring of what once had been sharply defined and hard.

He heard a quiet cough behind him and spun around, a hand reaching down to grab a non-existent sword. It was Jarz and he just given a disapproving look on seeing Jon's actions.

His voice was mildly irritated but mainly disappointed.

'Still looking for enemies, Jon? There are none here, how many times must I tell you this?'

Jon shrugged. 'I am not familiar with a world without enemies.'

Jarz said nothing for a few moments; his face almost unrecognisable without its trademark smile. Finally he said: 'Come with me please Jon.'

Jon saw no reason to refuse and so they went out into the bright warmth. Passing people hailed Jon as he walked on but perhaps slightly fewer than on previous occasions.

After a silent walk they came to a building that was distinctly larger than the usual with an impressive portico supported by a range of taller than normal columns. The portico had bas-reliefs carved into it which appeared to show men mounted on large quadrupeds pursuing a mass of fleeing pedestrians. Jon decided that he did not like the scene depicted but Jarz was urging him on.

They ascended a short flight of steps and came into a large room at the end of which was a block table behind which three men sat. Jarz stopped and withdrew very slightly.

'Jon this is the High Council. They would like to speak to you.'

Jon studied the three men. They looked older than any of the others he had met since arriving, the members of the latter all appearing to be the same age as Jon.

The middle man, a large, well-fed individual, spoke. 'Welcome to this meeting of the Council, Jon. I am Jolz2 and I am the Chairman.'

Jon nodded. 'I am pleased to meet you.' He wasn't but apparently it was the correct thing to say.

Jolz indicated a chair directly in front of the table and said, 'Please sit, Jon.'

Jon obeyed and an odd silence fell in which they stared at him and he stared back.

Finally the Chairman looked up from a paper in front of him and said, 'Jon, it seems to Jarz that you have an unusual attitude for a one so newly arrived. Having read his report, I am forced to agree.'

Jon swivelled his head to glare at Jarz who had occupied another chair behind him.

'You didn't tell me you were writing a report on me.'

The Chairman gave a slight coughing sound. 'Jon please, you must only address the Council when it is in session. Turn around please.'

Jon complied, changing the object of his stare to the Council.

The Chairman continued in defensive tones, as if he found the entire subject more than a little distressing.

'Now according to Jarz, since arriving you have done little else but go around questioning everyone that you meet and showing – it pains me to repeat this – very little gratitude for your fortunate position.'

Jon shrugged. 'I've asked a few questions. I would have thought that was normal for someone in a new situation.'

'But Jarz has already told you that all would be revealed to you in due time. '

Jon tried to control his growing irritation. 'The Gate of Light. What is it?'

The Chairman threw up his hands and glanced briefly at his companions.

'There you go again. Jon, if you are deemed worthy you will pass through the Gate of Light and meet your destiny. But this is not the time to contemplate that momentous day.'

'Why not?'

The Chairman leaned forward very slightly and when he spoke again his voice had hardened.

'Jon, precisely who do you think you are? You've fought your way out of a hostile environment and climbed a hill. Every man here has done exactly the same thing. What do you think makes you special? Come on – let's have it!'

Jon sat in silence with four pairs of eyes boring into him. Special. But strange to tell he did think he was special. From the

80

moment the great doubt had arisen in his mind he had felt that he had been marked out for something – something he knew not what.

'Is it delusional to feel that there are mysteries that need to be solved?' he finally said, not knowing where this vocabulary was coming from, 'To wonder what the purpose of this existence is?'

The Chairman rose. 'There are indeed mysteries. And they will be solved – but if you persist in this arrogance and impertinence they will not be solved by you.'

He turned to his silent fellow Councilmembers.

'Go.'

And with that, he raised both hands and looked up at some unseen thing in the ceiling.

'Now.'

And instantly a great, sonorous voice filled the room. A deep, strong voice with a timbre like rocks grinding together; a voice full of masculine power and confidence.

'Jon, I have been watching you. I like what I see. I like your speed, your power, your fortitude. It is indeed possible that one day you will sit at my right hand. But that time is not yet.

'Beware. I like the arrogance of ability, of puissance. But do not overreach yourself or you may yet learn fear when you see the approach of my fatal scimitar.'

Despite himself Jon was cowed. The voice had hit him like a physical blow, a great thrusting comber of solid sound breaking over him. It had taken all his will to avoid being tossed aside by it. What kind of being could speak in such a fashion?

He was only dimly aware that the Chairman had stopped glaring at him and vaguely saw him nod to someone behind Jon. Jarz came from behind him and, taking his arm, said gently, as if to a frightened child: 'Come on Jon. That's enough for today I think.'

Jon was aware that Jarz was leading him back out into the

81

skyshine; aware that the people in the streets were staring at him with concern in their faces instead of the usual pleasure. His self-awareness gradually came back as Jarz helped him along the street as if he were an invalid.

'Where are you taking me?' he muttered at last.

Jarz laughed. 'No need to worry Jon. I'm not taking you anywhere – except your home.'

True to his word, Jarz brought him into the house and tried to get him to lie on the bed but Jon refused.

'I don't like that thing' he managed to mumble.

Jarz nodded with the gentle concern of a parent. 'Of course. I'll leave you until tomorrow. I hope the next time we meet it'll be a little less tense now you've seen we're only here to help you.'

Jon did not watch him go; he simply wanted to be alone to think about what had happened. He had wanted something out of the routine to occur and his wish had been granted. But what had it meant? Who was the owner of that awful and awe-inspiring voice? And the warning – what was he being warned about?

And there was something else, something the voice had said, a phrase he remembered from somewhere, some other time. He shook his head. He could not bring the thing into his conscious mind.

He did little for the rest of the time of light. His evening meal appeared. Never had he seen it appear before his eyes or seen some low-status lackey bringing it in. He would turn away for a moment and when he turned back – there it would be. At exactly the right temperature and with the normal satisfying mix of textures and flavours. It was a wonder of course, but there were many wonders here. He didn't know how mirrors worked, for example – perhaps meals that appeared when no one was looking was a wonder of the same type. In this particular case, it was something to be accepted and not questioned. He definitely didn't want to go back to hunting kabarras.

He sat moodily in the chair by the table, morosely forking portions into his mouth of the rich brown substance he had encountered on his first day when he heard a slight movement at the doorway.

He leapt up and this time he was quick enough to see someone disappearing into the purple twilight. He looked down at the boundary between his dwelling and the outside world and, sure enough, there was another message lying there.

It read: "At first dayshine meet me at the twelfth house to your right."

* * *

With what felt remarkably like nervous anticipation Jon strode down the street. It would not be far to the designated meeting place and for some reason he didn't want to get there too quickly. He stopped and looked up. There shining softly and completely silently above him was the enigmatic pillar of light which from the start had marked out this hill as being unlike any other. Previous question-and-few-answer sessions with the locals had confirmed that this was indeed the fabled "Gate of Light." But what was it?

He remained still, staring at it until his neck began to ache. But the more he stared, the less he seemed to understand it. It was not solid, it was not smoke, it was not a collection of glowing particles caught in a great up draught. It was – just light. But an eerie, unknown light; a light which cast no shadows and altered when viewed with even a minute change in the angle of vision; sometimes soft and soothing; sometimes hard and harsh, with rays that struck like little needles flowing into the eyes. It sprang, as far as could be determined from below, from the bare rock of the summit but had no visible terminus, simply stretching up and up and up into invisibility, until the gaze was defeated by its vastness and returned to the surface. Nothing was visible within it or beyond it. It simply – *was*.

Jon gave up and continued to meet his mysterious confidant. He arrived at the designated house and was surprised to see that the door was shut. This was unusual in itself – doors were never shut in the village. The weather never changed and the people had no secrets, so why was this door shut? Having no experience of shut doors he hesitated in front of it, not sure what he was supposed to do. Then it opened and in the shadow a figure beckoned him in.

He followed it in, into a room very much like his own. The figure turned to face him and Jon had another electric shock that flashed down his spine.

He was looking at himself.

Well, not quite himself. What could be seen of the torso showed that it had none of the white, crisscrossing lines that the Lords of the Sands had left him. The face, too, was not quite the same. A little plumper in the cheeks perhaps, a few more lines in the forehead, perhaps. However, it was uncannily like the experience he had had with the mirror.

The figure spoke. 'I am Jon11 and you are Jon21.'

'I prefer just "Jon".'

The other smiled faintly. 'I understand that. I prefer just "Jon" as well. Take a seat.'

Jon did so, wondering if his voice really did sound like that. The other also seated himself and sat facing him, but not too close.

The stranger said after a short pause, 'I expect you're wondering what this is all about.'

'That's about right,' was Jon's dry reply.

'I believe you've just been through the magic show.'

'Magic show?'

'Let me get straight to it, the longer this takes the more danger we're in. Jarz took you to the council building where you were told that you'd been a naughty boy and that you'd better

84

buck your ideas up.'

'Something like that, yes.'

'And then you heard a terrible voice saying that someone had been watching you... and so on.'

Jon leaned forward eagerly. 'Yes! How do you know that?'

The other gave a world-weary smile. 'Because we've all been through it. Tell me, were there two other men there who didn't say anything and whose hands you never saw?'

Jon could not confirm the position of the hands but he could confirm the silence.

The other Jon nodded, with the expression of someone who had known all along that he was right but had just received indubitable confirmation.

'Naturally. They were the ones running the show.'

'The show – what show?'

'The voice, man! It's all an illusion, you didn't actually fall for it did you? It's just a normal voice somehow amplified – that means "made louder" – to scare you into submission. That's what they want – submission.'

Jon's face must have indicated incomprehension because Jon11 threw his hands up in disgust.

'The Council, man! They're running this place and they want us all to be good boys and do as we're told.'

'But we don't *do* anything here, except eat and sleep,' Jon observed, somewhat timidly.

'At the moment. But more of us are arriving every day. I know there's talk that when we reach a certain number something big is going to happen. You know about the Lords of the Sands?'

Jon started but simply replied 'Yes.'

'My bet is that we're going to go down and take their lands off them.'

'You've had dealings with them?'

'Not quite. They tried to capture me but I was too quick for them.'

Jon nodded. This sounded plausible but it didn't seem to account for all he had seen.

'What about the Gate of Light? Where does that come in?'

Jon11 snorted. 'The Gate of Light! That's another of their tricks! Does it look like a gate? And if you went through it you'd just be on the other side of the hill!'

'It doesn't look like anything I've ever seen before,' Jon observed mildly.

'You've seen everything there is, have you? It's just a natural thing, is all. Why is the sky red?'

'I don't know,' Jon admitted, 'But what about the Lord Korok?'

Jon11 burst into spluttering laughter. 'Man, they picked an easy target with you, didn't they? Korok - where is he? Have you seen him walking around, scratching his bum? Don't you get it — he's the biggest trick of all. A bogeyman to frighten us all so we do what we're told.

'There is no Lord Korok!'

Four

The excited voice trilled through the morning air.

'Today is the day! Today! The time of the hunt!'

Jon ignored the voice. He did not know what it meant and at that exact moment he did not care. He strode back and forth, clenching and unclenching his great hands.

How could he have been so stupid! It was now obvious that the whole meeting at the Council had been a sham, a simple box of tricks designed to fool the unsophisticated newcomer. And he had fallen for it!

The question was – what to do now? Should he simply ignore the whole thing and settle down to enjoy this simple life? After all, had he not deserved an easy time, with food and drink not merely on demand but suddenly appearing on his table before he had fully realised that he wanted them?

He continued his pacing, unable to resolve the issue. He disliked being made a fool of but what was the alternative – should he storm the Council building and attack the members with his bare hands?

Obvious nonsense.

He sat down and rested his chin on a fist. No answers came to him.

It was then that he became aware that it was becoming very noisy outside, with an excited babble getting louder and louder until it was unquestionably obtrusive. Feeling distinctly annoyed he rose and looked out of his door.

There was a throng of people stretching in all directions along the terrace. Some were looking very excited and were engaged in feverish conversations with their fellows; others were solitary, or at best in small groups, and looking very worried and dejected.

Jon stared up and down the crowd, trying to make sense of what was happening. Finally, he stopped a man who was rushing past his door and demanded: 'What's going on?'

The other made to pull himself out of Jon's grasp but it was too strong.

'It's the hunt, you yokel. Now let me go!'

Jon continued to hold the struggling man.

'Who is hunting who?' he demanded.

The man stopped his flailing and looked Jon full in the face.

'Why a Degenerate of course. Who else? Now let me go before I call a Councilman!'

Jon complied, not because of the threat but because of that word.

Degenerate.

Certain words and phrases kept recurring. They seemed to hold some great meaning, perhaps some dread meaning. But he did not know what that meaning was.

He watched the man hurry off without emotion or interest. He had no desire to get involved in whatever this foolish ceremony was. He was tired of this whole way of life; this repetition of meaningless trivia; of periods of light which were utterly indistinguishable from each other. The purgatory of the quiet life.

He realised then that he had in fact made his decision: coming here had been a mistake. He had condemned himself to a meaningless life where people in power obviously took him to be an ignorant dupe. Well no more!

He strode angrily back into his house. And then he stopped, rigid with astounded shock.

His sword was there, exactly where he had left it, all those periods of light ago.

He picked it up, turning it over and over, trying to make sure that it was indeed his sword, the one given to him by the Lords of the Sands. It was; he saw all the small nicks and blemishes in the unknown black material (had they said: "Midnight Steel"?) from which the Lords fashioned their weapons. It was his sword.

Jarz had said that he might get it back but had implied that there might be some unpleasantness involved in its return. No matter. Jon grasped the sword and waved it back and forth, feeling a welcome optimism flowing back into him.

He no longer felt naked and vulnerable. Let dangers come! He would face them now!

Now it was time to discover what was happening that had got the populace into such a turmoil.

Stepping outside, he saw that the crowd had got even larger and, if possible, even more agitated.

He hailed another passer-by, this time not so aggressively.

'This hunt – where is the Degenerate?'

The other had time to grin before rushing on.

'We'll find out soon. You'd better hope it's not you!'

A strange answer, Jon thought, surely either you were or were not a Degenerate – whatever that unfortunate state was. He decided to follow the retreating individual to see if he could discover more about this unknown ceremony.

The people seemed to be thinning out in one particular area and Jon shouldered his way through to see if anything special was visible. Nothing unexpected was, just more people, some looking around with what even at this distance was clearly terror.

Jon had just decided that he was wasting his time and, now that he had his sword, that it was time to begin his journey back to the forest when a shrill cry rang out: 'There it is! Here it comes!'

Jon spun around and saw a small ball of bright blue light soaring through the air towards him, moving as it were completely weightless. It passed close to the top of his head without giving any sensation of its passage. Jon spun around to follow its movements and saw it hover over one man directly in front of him. The man stared up at him, his features having

89

gained a weird bluish tinge from its radiance.

'Come on!' he yelled, 'I'm ready!' He had a short sword which he waved at the sphere in apparent defiance. The sphere remained motionless for a short time and then gave a small shivering movement, almost as if it were shrugging non-existent shoulders. It moved onto another, where a very similar scenario was enacted.

And then it stopped above another, who was very agitated. The man was some distance from Jon but it appeared that his features were contorted into a mask of fear and pleading.

Jon heard him cry 'No not me! What have I done! Leave me be!'

And with that he dropped his sword, turned and ran, the crowd parting to let him through, laughing as they did so. The small ball of light remained motionless for a moment and then swept after him. Jon followed, mystified by the whole performance but determined to discover its denouement.

Forcing himself through the resisting mass of onlookers Jon caught up with the fugitive at almost the same moment as the questing sphere. It descended on the man's head and then seemed to liquefy, running down his body in rippling cascades of swirling sapphire. The man screamed.

Then the crowd began to chant.

'Degenerate! Degenerate!' they chanted in ominous unison, 'Kill the Degenerate!'

The light abruptly disappeared from the apparent victim and as if no longer supported by an invisible rope he crashed to the ground and, on his knees, looked around and cried 'Please, I beg of you! Don't do this!'

A wave of laughter swelled up from the others and the circle of unoccupied ground around him shrank as they moved closer, their swords raised ominously high. Jon stared in amazed horror, his own sword pointing at the ground.

Another metronomic chant began with a very simple

message: 'Kill. Kill. Kill.'

And then the cutting began. They closed in on him and jabbed with their short swords, stabbing, withdrawing, stabbing. Patches of blood began to appear through his tunic, rapidly spreading. He screamed but this did not stop the rhythmic stabbing.

As the man writhed on the ground he managed to glimpse Jon and realising in his pain that Jon was not holding his sword in the stabbing position saw a possible saviour. He crawled towards Jon who stood transfixed, unable to advance or retreat.

He came so close to Jon that his outstretched hand almost touched Jon's foot with bloodied fingers.

Through a tumult of horror Jon heard the words: 'Help me!'

Jon could not move. His time with the Lords had made violence familiar to him but never had he seen such a vile display of sadistic terror inflicted on a totally helpless being. The Lords had only ever fought one on one, even if the final outcome had never been in doubt. So profound was his shock that he found he could not move; everything was as unreal as if he was in a nightmare from which there was no awakening - the widening pools of blood sinking into the ground; the look of uncomprehending horror in the victim's eyes, blinking as rivulets of blood ran over and into them. The lust-thickened chants of the crowds beat on his ears as he stood there, hesitant.

'Death to the Degenerate! Death to the Degenerate!'

And then Jon's indecision was rendered meaningless. There was one final thrust, one final groan and then the man lay silent and still.

A great roar of approval went up all around then, breaking into a thunderclap of crazed exultation. Jon did not attempt to listen to the words; he could guess their meaning without having to consciously take them in. Sheathing his useless sword, he turned abruptly and forced his way through the chanting throng, angrily pushing out of the way any who impeded his path.

In his room he sat with his back to the open door, vaguely aware that the shouting was gradually fading away. Why had he done nothing? Why had he not defended the man? What kind of man had he become?

He heard movement behind him and spun around, expecting the crowd to have followed him to taunt him. But it was Jarz.

The man's face was flushed and he was breathing heavily as if coming down from some unclean orgasm.

'Jon, wasn't that wonderful!' he gasped in a breathy voice, as if still too excited for normal speech, 'The way of the Degenerate!'

'What do you want here?' was the stony reply.

Jarz looked slightly startled by this unenthusiastic response and just a little hurt.

'Well I was intending to show you how to use the viewing device but I don't think I'll bother now.' He indicated the small device with the padded ends that Jon had wondered about earlier on in their acquaintance. Jon glanced at it and then turned back to stare at Jarz.

'Why was that man killed?'

Jarz shrugged. 'Obvious isn't it? He was a Degenerate.'

'Was he a Degenerate before that ball thing touched him?'

'He must have been. Do you think the Lord Korok makes mistakes? Have a care Jon.'

Jon leapt up and crossing the space between them in a blur of movement grabbed Jarz by the throat.

'Korok! Korok! Stop this stupid game! Either there is no Korok or you and the rest of that sick Council are Korok, hiding behind a shadow so you can play your vile games with human prey!'

With surprising strength Jarz tore Jon's hand away from his throat and stepped back.

'You go too far Jon, much too far. You've already been

92

warned, in what we thought were clear enough terms but it seems you are too stupid to understand what was said.

'You'll get no more warnings – the next time you step out of line it'll be actions – actions you won't like!'

With that he was gone.

Jon sat down heavily, choking in a mass of conflicting emotions – anger, guilt and just a little fear. He had earlier decided to leave – surely it was more obvious than ever that this place was some kind of trap. Now – he must go now!

It was then a great voice filled his room and his head, a deep, powerful voice as if colliding boulders could suddenly speak.

'Jon, Jon, you have disappointed me. I had great hopes for you; hopes that you could lead my vanguard. You had the chance to display courage and resolve, to show that you are not afraid to be magnificently cruel in my service to those who can only grovel and plead for mercy. But you backed away, you could not wield the fatal scimitar.

'But I will not abandon you, Jon. I sense greatness in you. I am certain you will achieve many things which are at present beyond your understanding. Therefore I will not cast you out.

'But you must be punished for your weakness, for that is the one sin which is above all others. This is your punishment. Accept it. Affirm it. And soon we will talk again.'

And with that, the voice ended and the pain began.

Licking tongues of fires ascended Jon's body and began invading his innards like flesh dissolving leeches. He felt as if molten metal was being sprayed over and into him. The world dissolved into a red opacity in which there was only pain. Pain piled high upon pain. Pain which laughed and shrieked as it explored his innermost being.

Then it ended leaving Jon limp and sweating on the floor. As he regained some semblance of control over his tremblings and shudderings he forced himself to his feet, thrust the sword into its scabbard and without a backward glance burst out of the door, He looked neither to the left or to the right but fixed his gaze firmly on the world which lay beyond the hill, the world to which he was returning.

But then he stopped. Someone was climbing over the lip of the terrace, someone who did not look like anyone he had ever seen before, a tall figure with a tumbling mass of amber-gold hair.

Five

Jon stared in fascinated puzzlement as the stranger drew nearer. Its point of entry to the village meant it was heading straight for him so he had plenty of time to study it.

There was something both odd and yet oddly familiar about this person. And then Jon realised: he was seeing one of the mysterious women-things close up. That explained the odd mixture of familiarity and difference.

He could clearly see now why those distant figures hadn't looked quite right; this person, although not far off Jon's height, had a somewhat different structure to the main part of their body and, although clearly of the same basic plan as everybody else, it looked softer somehow and designed by someone who was very fond of curves.

However, there was one very striking difference and Jon wondered for a moment whether this poor unfortunate was suffering from some kind of deformity. From the central part of the chest there were two fleshy mounds sticking out in a basically horizontal plane. They were certainly most unusual and as the person came right up to him Jon decided to see if they were as firm as they looked and, reaching out, he grasped the two mounds and began to squeeze them.

After he picked himself up off the hard ground he rubbed the sore part of his chin for a while whilst glaring at the stranger.

'Why did you hit me?' he asked, somewhat plaintively.

'Why did you touch me?' the stranger replied, having stepped back slightly from grasping or striking distance.

'I wanted to see if you were alright,' Jon said and began rubbing his bruised chin again.

The newcomer shrugged. 'I'm perfectly fine, no need to worry about me. But are you alright? I didn't mean to hit you that hard – you startled me, that's all.'

Jon felt that he was losing his hard-earned status somehow. 'I'm fine too. I've been hit a lot harder than that. You took me by surprise, that's all.'

The two stared at each other; eye to eye on nearly the same level.

Then finally the incomer spoke and her stony stare softened, ever so slightly.

'Let's start again. My name is Shana', and she extended a hand.

'And I'm Jon.'

Jon knew by now that he was meant to hold the hand and give it a quick shake, which he proceeded to do although he couldn't see why doing this to a hand was fine but doing the same thing to a flesh-mound was not. The hand had a calloused palm and the grip was firm. Jon had thought that he had mastered the intricacies of social intercourse, but apparently he had not. Only one way to find out.

'So to ask again – why did you hit me?'

And this time she gave a slight smile. 'You didn't ask. If you want to do that you must ask.'

'Can I touch you?'

'No.'

Jon looked skywards briefly. Time to move on.

'So you are a – woman?'

'I believe so. Although I've never met any others. I'm obviously different from you so I can only assume you're not a woman.'

Jon mulled this over. This confirmed his suspicions that people came in two different types. Was there another type? he wondered, after all there were three types of kabarra.

He gave her another stare, at which she put a hand on one hip and assumed a pained expression. He noticed that she had an enormous sword hanging by her side. Why hadn't he noticed

96

that before?

'You've had a bit of trouble, I see.'

'Just a bit. But they won't be giving anybody else any. I...'

She broke off and Jon turned around to see what she had noticed.

It was Jarz. He came rushing up, brushed past Jon, whom he totally ignored, and reached up to clasp Shana's shoulder whilst giving her his broadest smile. She very gently removed his hand and stared down at him. She definitely didn't like being touched, thought Jon.

'My dear, my dear, it's good to see you! Welcome, welcome to our little village!'

Shana extended a hand. 'Thank you. I'm Shana.'

'Yes, yes, I know. Shana12.'

She frowned slightly. 'No, just Shana.'

'My dear, you've only just arrived. There's a lot you have to learn but I'm sure that an intelligent girl like you will have no trouble fitting in.' At this point in his spiel he glanced back at Jon who was standing just behind him and to one side. 'But there's a slight problem.'

Shana's frown grew slightly more evident. 'Problem? I've only just arrived.'

'Yes, yes. It's nothing to worry about let me assure you. But you've come to the wrong part of our village.'

'In what way?'

'Well, this is actually the part of the village that is reserved for men. You'll have to go to the women's village.'

Shana spent a few moments absorbing the implication of Jarz's words: that she was not the only woman in the world. But then she looked up and said: 'Why?'

'Why? Well, my dear, it's the way we do things here. I...'

'I'm not your "dear",' Shana said, abruptly cutting him off in full flow, 'I've come a very long way. I've killed a number of things that were trying to kill me. I'm tired. I want to rest. I have

97

no intention of going to any other part of the village, however near that may be.'

Jarz looked completely dumbfounded. 'But there's no place for you to stay here. It's' …

Shana turned from him to Jon, who had been standing there enjoying Jarz's growing puzzlement and discomfort.

'I'm sure Jon here will be able to put me up. Am I right Jon?'

Jon felt a strange electric tingle flash through his body at the thought of having company in his dwelling. For a moment he couldn't form any words and then said 'Yes. There's room. Or I can make room, depending on how much you need.'

Shana smiled and the electric tingle returned to Jon, but stronger.

'We can work something out. You don't look like the kind of man who is easily discouraged.'

Jon felt then as if whatever Shana wanted he would do his best to provide. A small part of his mind whispered to him: You've only just met her. Why are you doing this?

But he ignored that very small part of his mind.

Jarz stepped between them, reserving his glare for Jon.

'Don't do this. It will not be at all liked by …'

'Don't say it,' said Jon, raising a finger and placing it a very short distance from the tip of Jarz's nose, 'just don't say it.'

* * *

Shana and Jon faced each other in his house with Jon marvelling how his guest seemed to have been poured onto the chair, while he was simply sitting stiffly on his. She had pulled a loose green blanket over her, for as the time of light drew on she had observed that it was distinctly colder than in the lands of her recent experience.

Jon was fascinated to hear of the Land from which she had come and on how nothing threatened any other thing but lived together in a harmonious world of warmth, plenty and gentleness. How different from my forest! he thought somewhat bitterly, as the memories of being stalked by the ferocious night predators came unpleasantly back into his mind. And the endless search for elusive kabarras. How wonderful it must be to simply dip one's hand into the river and pull out a fat food fish!

As far as he could determine his guest had come from precisely the opposite direction to his. She knew nothing of the Lords of the Sands, from which Jon determined that their territory must be strictly limited in area and did not form an encircling ring around the hill. His eyes narrowed when she talked of Zarka and Akraz and the conundrums that they had forced her to confront, wishing he had been there to allow them to taste the bitter blackness of his sword.

She had just finished relating the final one that they had set her when a little light of devilment came into her eyes.

'And what is the solution Jon? A worldly-wise person such as yourself must be able to grasp it at once.'

Jon went very still. For reasons he could not express, he had found himself wishing to impress her in everything he said or did. The sensible thing would have been to confess his inability for, if the truth be told, he hadn't even been able to solve the first problem.

But although he didn't know why, he wasn't feeling entirely sensible.

'It's ... it's ...' he said, very slowly.

Shana cocked her head slightly to one side.

'Yes?' she murmured sweetly.

'It's ...'

'It's to do with the problem of self-reference. That's what you were going to say, wasn't it?'

Jon wasn't sure whether she was setting a playful trap for him but decided to take a chance.

'Yes. That's exactly it.'

She clapped her hands. 'There – I knew you'd understand!'

Jon was amazed by how much relief he felt at that. He hadn't felt anything like it since the Lords had decided to spare his life.

She stood up in a single fluid, graceful movement and wrapped the blanket more tightly around her. She moved towards the open door, feeling the cooling air wash over her in gentle ripples.

'It's not like the Land here but it has its beauty.'

Jon nodded wisely though the concept of his surroundings being "beautiful" had never crossed his mind.

She moved closer to the doorway.

'It seems peaceful here. Looking down on everything. Admiring the deep green sky.'

Jon looked up sharply at that comment. He had thought that he and the woman had been able to establish a complete understanding when they spoke to each other. His language and hers had seemed to have been identical up to this point.

He joined her at the doorway.

'That's odd,' he said, 'you use a different word than we do.'

She turned. 'In what way?'

'Well you use the word "green" and we use the word "red."'

A frown crinkled her otherwise unblemished forehead.

'What are you talking about?'

He held her shoulder (without asking permission) and turned her so she was looking directly at the sky.

'The sky - it's what we call red.'

'Jon, I know what red is. The sky is not red.'

Jon gave a tolerant smile and pulled the blanket a little way from her bare shoulders.

'Shana. This is what we call "green".'

Her expression, at first bemused, was beginning to show unmistakeable signs of irritation. Jon began to wonder what he had done wrong now.

'That's what I call green too. The sky is green!'

Jon's expression changed as well, from tolerance to somewhat worried concern. Had he offered to share his house with a madwoman?

He tried again.

'Tell me what you see.'

'I see a deep green sky. And just now the circle that means the time of darkness is coming has appeared at the zenith.'

Jon stared up.

He saw no circle.

He said, very slowly and carefully, 'Do you not see a deep red sky with bands of purple beginning to show?'

'No I do not.'

Jon went back into the room and sat down, deep in thought.

And then he looked up and said, slowly and carefully, 'Shana, there is something wrong with The Universe.'

Six

They sat staring at each other, unable to speak, almost unable to think. Vague, inchoate thoughts swirled muddily in their minds, refusing to come to a stop, refusing to settle, refusing to clarify. Doubts which had had no form, no substance, now rose to dominate their thinking. What was this world they inhabited? And more to the point, what was their role in it?

Shana spoke first. She lifted her head and Jon was taken aback to see the lines of worry drawn harshly across her face, twisting it into the face of someone he hardly knew.

'Have you had doubts about this world of ours?' she whispered.

Jon nodded. 'Yes. Just before that compulsion to leave the forest came upon me. I had them.'

'And what did you doubt?'

'Little things which I had never noticed before. The way the creatures in the forest seemed clumsy, awkward…' he hesitated for a few moments, searching for the words, the concepts, 'they looked – badly designed.'

She nodded. 'I thought the same things about the creatures in the Land. It did not seem possible that they could be independent living things. Not like me. I have structure, a complexity which they lacked. And like you, I suddenly came to that realisation. It was if a curtain had been drawn.'

He said nothing but stared at her impassively, waiting for her to still his tumbling thoughts.

She continued: 'And the more you look, the more you see.' She reached across the narrow space between then, touching his arm as a child looking for comfort might touch its parent. 'Have you ever wondered why it is that we take things into our bodies, food, water, but nothing comes out?'

He hadn't but as soon as she had said it the absurdity of the situation hit him like a physical blow.

'Yes, of course. How can that be possible? If you put objects in a carrying bag there comes a time when no more can go in. But that doesn't happen to us. Or anyone else for that matter.'

He thought of the Lords of the Sands and how he had found their physical form somewhat absurd. And they too had eaten and drunk without consequences.

Shana had developed a look he didn't like; a troubled, hunted expression that sat badly on her.

'Something is wrong,' she muttered, looking around the room as if the answer lay somewhere within it, 'something badly wrong.'

Silence fell again as they realised that they faced an existential issue beyond their abilities to unravel.

The silence was broken by a sharp knock on the side of the doorway. Jon sprang up to see who was calling at this hour of the time of darkness.

A figure came in and the flickering light revealed it to be Jon11.

Shana sprang to her feet, disconcerted by the appearance of a near-identical copy of the man she was with.

'Who is this?' she gasped, turning to her original companion.

'I'm Jon11,' the other answered, 'I'd heard that there was a woman in our part of the village and I came to see if the story was true.'

'As you can see,' Shana stated, somewhat brusquely, 'it is true. Is that all?'

Jon11 pulled out another chair and sat down, casually inspecting Shana as he did so.

'Not quite. As you're a newcomer here I thought I'd make sure you know what's going on here before the rulers manage to fill your head with nonsense.'

'Nonsense?' she inquired, glancing at the original Jon.

'Yes, nonsense. I'm afraid your friend here, a somewhat damaged version of me, thinks we are all under the control of some invisible entity that can look into men's minds and punish them for thoughts he doesn't like.'

Jon stood up and looked down on his twin.

'After the slaughter out there – the so-called "Degenerate Hunt" - I was made to feel excruciating pain, pain like I'd never known before. And I heard the voice again – warning me.'

Jon11 shrugged. 'Do you think we are dealing with amateurs here? They saw your reaction out there. And they're not the only ones. I saw it too and couldn't believe how stupid you were to let your feelings be exposed so easily. If you want to overthrow them, man, you'll have to be just a little more covert, to be able to undermine them from within.'

'And the pain? How do you explain that?'

The other shrugged again. 'I didn't follow you here but they have poisons which cause both hallucinations and physical suffering. I've seen it done. No doubt someone nicked you with a poisoned blade as you rushed past in your panic.'

Jon stood still. It all sounded so reasonable. It could easily have happened, just the way Jon11 was describing it.

'It could have happened,' he said hesitantly. His head was beginning to spin again. Nothing stood still; nothing was certain. Everything was dissolving into a flux of madness.

Jon11 looked sharply at Shana. 'And you? Do you believe in things you can't see, can't touch but somehow they know what you're doing and can punish you for your innermost thoughts?'

She looked helplessly at her housemate. 'It does seem – unlikely.'

'Good.' Jon11 looked and sounded pleased with his evening's work. 'Now that we've got that out of the way perhaps I can get you two to work with me so we can finally get things done around here. So let's hear no more about Mr. Bogeyman – or should I call him "Lord Korok"?'

104

Shana was already standing but she suddenly seemed to grow taller as every muscle in her lithe body instantly went iron rigid.

'Korok? Lord Korok?' she yelled, in a voice that shook the rafters.

Both Jons were startled and after a moment's stunned silence Jon11 said, almost meekly, 'That's the name they've given him.'

She looked at the other Jon almost accusingly.

'Why didn't you tell me about him?' she demanded.

'I thought I had.'

She began to pace back and forth in front of the bemused Jons.

'Lord Korok, Lord Korok,' they heard her mutter to herself, 'Akraz, Zarka. The prison in the hills. The fatal scimitar.'

Suddenly she turned on Jon11, blue-grey eyes blazing. 'Get out you fool, get out! Whatever the Lord Korok is, he's no daydream, no fantasy. Get out!'

* * *

The departure of their uninvited guest had done nothing to restore equanimity to Jon and Shana. If anything, it had heightened their discomposure; the feeling of crawling unease that lurked behind every thought.

Realising that in the apparent excitement at learning about each other as persons that they might have overlooked vital elements in their past experiences, they went over those experiences in great detail. It seemed to Jon that he stood there in the cave as Shana writhed on the floor, desperately getting closer and closer to the weapon that might save her. Shana stood shoulder to shoulder with Jon as he strove against the champions of the Lords of the Sands.

There were differences in their experiences: Shana had

merely been told of Korok's existence while Jon had somehow had the notion buried in the depths of his mind.

Both agreed that the entity known by that name was held in great respect, not to say awe, by the others who knew of him. Jon11 must be wrong to claim that he was simply an abstract figurehead chosen by the Council to frighten the populace into submission. Somehow, someway, there must be a reality behind that name; a great and terrible reality that turned men into whimpering slaves.

Jon recalled that when he had heard the great voice it had not overtly stated that it was Korok who had been speaking, but who else could it have been? Only someone who had the power to terrify men could have produced tones such as he had heard.

Impasse. They stopped their talking and gazed at each other helplessly. They had determined beyond all reasonable doubt that there was a Korok and he was a terrible danger to them but, worse than that, a danger that could not be outfaced; a danger beyond the reach of the sword.

'What can we do?' Shana eventually said.

Jon shook his head. 'I don't know.'

To leave the hill must be the most obvious course of action but Korok's reach was not confined to this immediate vicinity, for the Lords of the Sands had known of him and feared him; Akraz had spoken of him with humble respect. And Jon was reminded that Korok seemed to have a personal interest in him. No, flight was not the answer.

Eventually they both stood up as if controlled by one impulse and put their arms around each other's shoulders.

Eyes nearly on the same level stared into each other.

'We'll find a way out of this,' was Jon's eventual comment.

Shana gave a welcome smile that restored her features to the way they had looked when Jon had first seen them.

'Yes we will,' she said and kissed him.

It was not a long kiss but to Jon it was as if he was suddenly swimming in a warm sea of achingly pleasurable wonder.

He leaned forward to renew the experience but Shana had turned away, not having noticed his state of excitement.

She had picked up the implement with the padded ends.

'What is this?'

Jon confessed his ignorance.

'Jarz was going to show it to me but as he doesn't appear to like me any more it looks like I'll never know.'

Shana turned it over and over in her strong hands.

'It looks like – yes it does!'

She had placed the padded ends of the implement over her ears and pushed the flexible band down so it had disappeared into her riotous locks.

Immediately she staggered and Jon was forced to catch her to prevent her crashing to the floor.

'What is it?' he demanded anxiously.

She tore the thing off her head.

'I don't know. For a moment I seemed to see pictures in my head. Things that looked as real as this room but then they were gone.'

He sat her down and then looked dubiously down at the object as he held it at arm's length.

'Perhaps I should try it.'

Very slowly and carefully he lowered it upon his head as he had seen Shana do and sat down next to her. He remained stock-still for an increasingly worrying length of time, eventually forcing Shana to vigorously shake his arm.

'Jon! Jon! What is it? What are you seeing?'

He took it off and placed it on the table next to them.

'I didn't see much. For a moment there were people and then just blackness.'

'Blackness. Just blackness?' *This didn't seem particularly interesting*, she thought.

Jon did not look at her but just sat there, slowly rubbing his chin.

'Well, not entirely black. In different places there were little lights, little unblinking lights.'

Shana sat up straighter. 'Little lights, so small that you couldn't see any detail in them – as if they were just incredibly small points?'

'Yes – I suppose that's the best way of describing what I saw. But nothing was happening. Just blackness and the little lights.'

But Shana was no longer listening. This was one of her dreams and now Jon had seen it.

This must be significant; it must be part of the answer to the dilemma that they had found themselves embedded in. Any small increase in their understanding might be enough to spring the jaws of their trap and let them out into a world of sanity.

Shana picked up the device and put it back in the alcove from whence it had been taken.

'Jon, it's very late. We must rest. We don't know what we will have to face tomorrow. But,' and here she glanced back into the alcove, 'that thing is part of the answer we are looking for. But we can't take it any further now. But tomorrow...'

And they slept.

* * *

As the new period of light came into existence Jon and Shana reviewed their situation. No great insights had come to them during the period of darkness; there had been no astounding dream that had explained all the mysteries and contradictions that swirled around them.

They were just as they had been before.

But they could not shed the unsettling revelations that had come to them.

As they ate their breakfast Jon moodily considered the fact

that although he still felt hungry before the meal and felt energised after it, the simple act of eating was now a mystery. Whereas before there had just been a simple act, now there was – mystery.

Somehow, whatever forces lay behind their meal arrangements knew that there were now two mouths to feed because two bowls of food appeared at the start of every new period. Shana did not comment on their dining arrangements; it was evident that one could have too many mysteries.

They decided that before there was any further discussion of their encircling problems they would check on the situation outside in the village.

They walked a little way from the house and it became immediately apparent that people were avoiding them. If someone happened to pass near, their gaze was directed to the left, to the right, to the ground, to the sky – never to them. Gone were the greetings called out as people saw them; gone were the smiles.

'This must be what it is like to be some kind of plague carrier,' Jon observed morosely, as the twentieth person made a wide detour so as not to pass near them.

'We are plague carriers, Jon. We carry the plagues of doubt and disobedience.'

Despite the invisible barrier that the two seemed to carry with them, Jon noticed that there were more people around than he had seen before. And even as he looked casually around two men came over the lip of the terrace and were immediately surrounded by happy welcomers.

'Something's happening,' he said, 'there're more people here now than this village can hold.'

Shana did not comment - she was looking up at the sky, wondering that although it looked green to her, to Jon it was crimson.

Thus it was that they did not see Jarz as he came up to them and blocked their way.

When Jon did finally see him, he snapped, 'And what now? More warnings?'

Jarz's face was like stone.

'As a matter of fact, yes. Our Lord is disturbed by you Jon and,' and here he turned to glare at Shana 'especially by you.'

'Really?' was her laconic reply.

'It is not a matter for levity,' Jarz hissed, and his voice became suddenly quiet as if he feared that someone was listening, 'You do not understand the power that could be brought against you. Not the Council, that is just a small matter in your fates. But here we are all in the grasp of the Lord Korok; he has our lives in his hands. He can do with us as he wishes; we are just clay he can mould, make and shatter. He can kill us in an instant, yes and resurrect us and kill us again and again!'

Although outwardly unmoved, both Jon and Shana were shaken by this vision of their utter helplessness.

'And what does he want from us?' Jon finally muttered.

'You must give yourself over to him completely. You must cease this questioning and wondering and accept that all you need to know comes from the Lord Korok. He knows your thoughts and he disapproves.'

'And you know this – how?' said Shana, her eyes flashing with what was now explicit contempt.

'Because I have seen others like you who thought to put themselves above the Lord and I saw what happened to them. And there is another thing.'

'Which is?' she continued.

Jarz's voice dropped its sacerdotal quietness and a note of triumph entered it.

'Look around! See how many of us there are now. Soon there will be enough for our army to cross into the Gate of Light!'

Seven

Jon and Shana did not stay much longer outside in the village after their encounter with Jarz. There was little point in doing nothing but watch themselves being avoided by large numbers of people and in any case, his words lay heavy on their minds.

For the first time the unpleasant word "army" had been uttered with the implication that this army would soon be employed against some unknown foe. The Gate of Light was somehow the key to understanding what was about to happen but still they had no idea what that strange object was or what its role would be.

So many questions.

So few answers.

So they sat, dispirited, enervated, facing an existence beyond their understanding and which had revealed itself to be implacably hostile to them.

It was Shana who broke the silence.

'We must do something, anything.'

Jon shrugged, not even looking at her. 'What's the point. Nothing we can do will make any difference.'

She stood up and walked over to the alcove and picked up the strange device.

'You said Jarz was going to train you in the use of this.'

'Yes.'

'Then it must be important. The very fact that he has now refused to tell you any more about it proves that.'

She held it out to him.

'Put it on.'

He glanced up at her listlessly, saw the determination in her eyes and finally obeyed.

Moment after moment went by and he did not move, did

not speak.

Finally, irritated by the silence and immobility, Shana snapped, 'Well what do you see? Is there something wrong with you?'

He took the device off and put in on the nearby table, moving slowly as if it were incredibly heavy.

'Nothing. I saw that blackness again and the points of light. Then nothing.'

She frowned. 'There's something wrong. Jarz wouldn't have refused to say any more about it if it's just a silly toy. Here, let me have it.'

She placed it on her head and closed her eyes.

And waited.

For some time nothing happened and then gradually, very gradually, images began to form, images of things she could not quite understand.

She saw the sky but a sky with a most peculiar colour, neither green nor red but a pale blue and in it or on it were impossible things – great white masses like floating mountains, things that could not possibly exist.

She saw buildings, but not buildings such as the village possessed; but tall, enormous structures seemingly comprised of stone, of metal and material that was totally transparent. In the air there were great flying things, also of similar materials to the buildings; flying things so vast that it seemed completely impossible that they could lift themselves into the air.

And the people! So many people!

How could there be room for all these multitudes!

There were endless roads with metal boxes travelling along them at speeds so vast that she could not keep them fixed in her vision. Everywhere there were the signs of huge numbers of people in a great hurry, of things to do, of journeys that must be made.

It was too much. Despite being immersed in the visions she

112

could feel the unknown implement resting on her head and so she took the thing off and slumped back in the chair.

Jon reached over and held her hands, 'What's wrong? You only had it on for a moment.'

She looked up at him in wonderment. His face seemed blurred.

'A moment? That's ridiculous!'

She told him of the things she had seen but it was obvious from his face that he did not understand. She gave up trying to describe huge flying things and said, 'I must go back in.'

'Why,' said Jon, concern clearly marked in his expression and in his voice, 'how do you know what you're seeing means anything? It all sounds like some kind of dream.'

'It means something,' Shana replied firmly, 'I must see more.'

And she did.

The scenes became more disturbing. There was a feeling of crisis in the way the ant-like communities were behaving. There was tumult in the streets beneath the tall buildings. Some groups were using violence against other groups. There were flames in the buildings, the boxes on the roads stopped moving, huge numbers of people were on the move, some coming into the great villages but more going out, in great waves of desperation. Huge encampments sprang up where displaced people lived in squalor. Some flying things fell from the sky and crashed into the ground in great billows of flame.

Shana saw all this as if she were a god. Sometimes she observed it from high above as if she were floating in the sky; sometimes she was there in the streets, seeing people running with fear and blood on their faces; sometimes great masses of stone fell on her from disintegrating buildings but left no mark. Like an all-seeing ghost, she walked among the terrified multitudes. Sometimes she would descend to a cellar where a frightened family huddled among the ruins of their possessions and the last of their bags of food, hearing the children cry and watching the adults hold each other. Then she would be watching hordes of men shaking what could only be weapons while behind them great metal boxes moved ominously forward, sending jets of flame and thunder to the left and to the right.

Something uniquely terrible was happening; some great overthrow of a peaceful society by forces that lusted for death and rejoiced in cruelty.

Then she heard a great voice that thundered from horizon to horizon and echoed and re-echoed around her.

'Now behold the fate of the Degenerates!'

Then there was a great light, a terrible flash so bright it was beyond description, a light so bright that had she been flesh it would have reduced her to whirling black flakes of carbon to be swept aside by a great wind. A horrible cloud of flame-shot blackness climbed implacably into the sky.

She screamed in a voice that came from the innermost depths of her being.

And then unconsciousness took her.

* * *

She awoke to find Jon staring down at her with lines of worry etched deeply into his face.

She was on the bed covered in sweat even though it was not particularly hot. Somewhere inside her skull something was bringing a hammer down, again and again.

Her mouth was dry but eventually she was able to ask: 'Have I been here long?'

Jon nodded. 'I was beginning to worry that you'd never wake up. You screamed and I pulled the thing off but you just lay there, unmoving.'

She swung her legs over the side of the bed and forced herself upright. 'Water. I must have water.'

114

As she sipped she began to feel better but the memory of what she had seen was like an invisible menacing presence in the room.

She related her visions even though it was quite clear that he wasn't understanding (or maybe not believing?) all she was saying.

'It's a different world, Jon. They are scenes from some other form of existence.'

Jon shrugged. 'What does that mean? How is it even possible? The world is the world. Where would this other one be?'

She began to pace up and down. 'We both agree that what we experience here doesn't make sense; as if it's not properly formed. Maybe what I'm seeing is a world that is properly formed!'

He was silent. She carried on, feeling almost desperate in her need to convince him.

'Look, this – this visualiser is important. Jarz said you were not ready for it which means it has some great significance in this village, some kind of truth that only people of a certain level are allowed to grasp. You upset this place's rulers and so it has been denied you.'

'Why didn't they take it away like they took our swords?'

'Because it seems that without the training it doesn't show you very much.'

'And you – who don't have any training – you can see all these things? Things that don't make any sense.'

She didn't say anything for a moment and then: 'It must be that I am some kind of person who is by chance attuned to it – some kind of natural user.'

She caught Jon raising an eyebrow.

'What - you think it's all make-believe? That I'm being fooled by some silly toy?'

He spread his hands in overt confusion. 'Is that less likely than what you've described. White mountains in the sky? Flashes of light that somehow can kill thousands of people?'

She sat still, suddenly assailed by doubt. Jon's objections had hit home– nothing she had described seemed at all likely, or even possible. And yet ... and yet...

Then she made up her mind. 'No, it means something. Something very important. Something that if we can only understand it will make sense of all this nonsense.

'And I'm going to keep going in until I find it.'

* * *

Despite what she had said Shana could not face another immersion in the visualiser so soon after her previous experience. She had to get out, to see her green cloudless sky, to escape the narrow confines of a building that was becoming more and more like a prison.

Reluctantly Jon agreed, seeing how profoundly she had been shaken by the things she had seen. But he insisted that they must take their recently returned swords with them every time they ventured out into the village for it was obvious that the hostility towards them was increasing steadily.

So it was that they went outside, expecting to be faced with the usual blank stares and indifference. But no! the village was in turmoil again and everyone they met appeared to be rushing in the same direction as if some great event was about to unfold.

Jon managed to stop one of the men as he hurtled by and despite the latter's clear reluctance to speak to him managed to get some information.

'The Council Building,' the man spluttered, 'got to get to the Council Building! Got to see it!'

Jon glanced at Shana and she nodded in silent agreement.

They arrived at the building to find a great throng already assembled and were not surprised to find them in great excitement, having heard their babble from some distance away. Everyone assembled seemed anxious to avoid physical contact with them and so it was easy for them to find their way to the front of the crowd, as it parted instantly to allow them through. But when they reached the front they were shocked to see what was revealed.

It was Jon11 and he was tied to a tall pole directly in front of the steps. Despite his condition his head was held high and he stared defiantly at his audience who by now were jeering and mocking him.

'You fools!' he yelled, 'don't you see you're next? You're next!'

Then the Chairman appeared from inside the building, descended the steps and stood in front of Jon11 and, after holding up a hand to quell their shouting, began to address the crowd.

'Men of the village!' he said in a solemn voice that was clearly audible now that an expectant silence had fallen, 'we have assembled here today for a great occasion. One that although regrettable is I'm afraid necessary and unavoidable. This ingrate,' and he turned briefly to glance at Jon11, 'has been spreading lies about our great Lord Korok. Lord Korok is just, merciful and patient. But there are some sins which cannot go unpunished. Jon11 has gone beyond the bounds of civilised life and must pay the penalty. Normally the punishment would be that he would be forbidden to enter the Gate of Light but for his crimes that will not be enough.'

A frisson of excitement rippled through the crowd. It was evident that they knew what that punishment would be. Shana looked helplessly at Jon but he shook his head. He did not know.

The Chairman turned to stare directly at Jon11.

'Well,' he said in a flat, disinterested tone, 'do you have anything to say? It may not be too late to cry out to Lord Korok for mercy.'

Jon11 tried to look past the Chairman's bulk to the hushed crowd beyond.

'Listen to me people! You have been lied to! Maybe I haven't got all the answers, maybe I've got some things wrong but my message is still the same! The Council is not your friend; you are being used for some purpose which is not clear but cannot possibly be for your wellbeing. Korok? Maybe there is a man called Korok hiding somewhere but he is not on your side – I tell you again. Look past all these tricks. Something is wrong! You are being used!'

Suddenly Jarz and another man broke from the first row of onlookers and bound Jon11's mouth. His pleas became first muffled and then completely inaudible. The other man and Jarz then returned into the crowd; somewhat hurriedly Jon thought.

The Chairman also increased his distance between himself and the captive. Then he looked up into the sky, raised both hands and cried: 'Now!'

And then it happened. A great column of blue-white heat descended with Jon11 at its exact centre. He writhed madly for a few desperate moments and then slumped as his skin was blackened and torn away. A great breaker of blistering heat crashed over Jon and Shana as in horrified fascination they watched the execution unfold before them. After the skin the musculature was dissolved revealing the inner organs, then just the bones, which when relieved of connective tissue fell in a calcined pile to the ground.

Shana screamed. She was the only member of the crowd to do so.

It was not over. The bone pile grew translucent, then transparent and finally blew away in a few curls of bluish vapour. The ground was empty.

The crowd dispersed, its members chattering excitedly to each other as they departed. Only Jon, Shana, the Chairman and Jarz were left. The Chairman lingered for a moment, discussing

118

something with Jarz and then left without a backward glance. Jarz glared at them for a while; looked like he was going to say something but then apparently thought better of it and marched off.

Only Jon and Shana remained, shaken to the core and with their arms around each other as they tried to forget what they had witnessed. But then Shana lifted her head and looked back at the pole. 'Something wrong,' Jon heard her murmur before she crossed to where Jon11 had died. He followed her and watched her crouch down on the ground, pressing her palms onto the soil. She looked up.

'Jon, we felt the heat. We saw what it did. But look – the ground. There's no trace of any damage. It's as if nothing has happened. That's not possible.'

Jon looked down at where she was pointing. She was right – there was not the slightest sign of any disturbance.

She stood up. 'Let's get back.'

They returned to the house in total silence, stunned into muteness by the enormity of the recent past. But the silence did not last.

No sooner had they arrived back when the building shook to a great voice, a voice like splintering stone.

'Jon. Shana. You have displeased me. You did not glory in the overthrow of an enemy. That is weakness and weakness is something I will not tolerate. But as you have not spoken out against me as Jon11 did, I will be merciful. Your punishment will be mild: I will not allow you to enter the Gate of Light with my army. Your days will be spent here, alone, in an empty village where you will have to scrabble for every speck of food, search for every drop of water.

'And Shana. I know of your movements in the world of the visualiser, which you have entered without my permission. But I will wait to see what transpires. It may be that from what you see and discover, wisdom may come to you in a way that it cannot

119

come to your companion.

'But beware: I watch you always.'

And with that, silence fell.

Eight

'You must not go back into the visualiser,' Jon told Shana.

She stared stonily back at him. 'And why is that?'

'You know why. Korok knows you're in there and he doesn't like it.'

Shana stretched her long limbs where she was lying on the bed. 'And tell me something he does like – apart from glorying in the death of an enemy, that is. No, he did not forbid me to use it; in fact, he said I might learn wisdom. Perhaps I will.'

'And do you want Korok's brand of wisdom?'

'I want the opportunity to find out more, so I can escape from this madness. Jon, you and I both know that what we're seeing can't be all there is. It's like some kind of puppet show with Korok pulling the strings.'

Jon had not seen a puppet show but he was able to guess her meaning.

'Maybe what you'll see will make you like Korok – despising weakness, glorying in suffering.'

She gave a sad smile. 'Do you know so little of me, Jon? Do you think that I could become like that?'

She got off the bed, came to him and ran warm fingers over his weary face.

'You and I are swords from the same forge Jon but we do not kill for the love of slaughter - only to defend ourselves from those who have that lust. Trust me.'

He smiled under the touch of her slim fingers. 'I do. You must do what you think is right. I can't go with you. You must go in there alone.'

They kissed again; this time with a sad gentleness.

* * *

121

Shana was immersed in the world of the visualiser. But this time there were not the terrible scenes of people hiding, running, dying. When the images stabilised they were of the interior of some large building made of material she did not recognise, a building in which she appeared to be entirely alone. She was in a long corridor between high walls that had many shelves on them. On the shelves were rectangular objects.

She selected the nearest and was surprised to see it fall open, revealing many thin sheets that had marks on them which she recognised as words. On the first page there were many words, with those at the top bigger and blacker than the rest. Shana was not surprised to discover that she could read the words: she had known that she would.

They said: **The Conquest of The Degenerates – Vol 1.**

She read some pages but found that her understanding was not as great as she had assumed; there were words there that she could not interpret except that they appeared to be referring to various places. Some were a type of village, but much, much bigger than the one she was in. Others referred to entire areas that held many villages. The names were strange; tongue-twistingly strange.

America.

Europe.

In her travels through the savage lands, none of her enemies had spoken of these places. Where could they be?

She read on:

"The so-called civilisation of the Degenerates suffered from many flaws but some in particular proved terminal. The culture placed an inordinate emphasis on tolerance and compassion, both proclivities being inimical to the development of the warrior spirit. In its final days, a culture of competitive compassion developed with groups seeking to outdo the other in their caring for others. A belief that the highest virtue was tolerance instead of the manly spirit of struggle was inculcated without pausing to consider where the unthinking tolerance of the intolerant would lead."

Shana stared at the words: she had no idea what they meant. The writer appeared to be scornful of the idea of caring for others, somehow believing that it was a fatal flaw in the survival of a society. But what would replace such an attitude? Shana had met many things in her travels that had wished her harm. She for her part had not wished them harm but had been forced to despatch them when their intentions had become plain.

Could there not be a compromise between compassion and self-interest? The writer clearly thought not: but surely nothing truly human could think that!

There was much more in the book, mostly claiming that the Degenerates had destroyed their own world from within by insidious cowardice and had deserved the punishment that had come upon them by those that were strangers to fear. She grew rapidly tired of it and read no more of the books in that section.

She looked around. Now she was used to the visons they seemed entirely real. She was dimly aware of the pressure of the device upon her head but she could see nothing of the room she was in or Jon's concerned face. The feeling that she was alone in a long corridor could not be distinguished from reality and although she had no physical sensation of her feet touching the floor, she could make herself walk down it.

It was a mysterious, incredible experience – but she was getting used to those now.

She rounded a bend in the corridor and saw that it opened up into a wide room without flanking bookshelves. At the far end, so distant that she could not make out the details, there was what appeared to be a table with a solid front. There were words on that front but they were so small it was hard to interpret them. One word was in larger characters and might have been "FORBIDDEN." She was about to approach when she saw movement. Her eyes narrowed. At either end of the table stood two short, squat figures. They were only silhouettes but their outline, their movements, reminded her of – Akraz and Zarka!

Her heart seemed to fly into her mouth as she hurriedly backed away, back into the sheltering corridor. No! No! her mind screamed; I can't face them again!

Back in the corridor she felt her pounding heart gradually return to its usual intensity. Perhaps she imagined it all. In this world where nothing was normal, a mind reeling under endless mysteries would overreact in some way – perhaps that was inevitable.

She looked carefully around the corner, ensuring that nothing below her eyes was visible to anything on the other side.

The table was still there but there were no figures. Her overwrought senses must have imagined them; imagined a horror coming back to taunt her.

However, she decided not to examine that area today. She began to retrace her steps. She knew it was unnecessary and that she was in fact lying motionless on the bed but it was hard to shake the illusion that she was actually walking back to an entry point. As she did so she noticed a book that had a brightly coloured spine, unlike the dull tan of most of the others.

She took it off the shelf, having to stand tiptoe to do so, and read the title:

THE WAY OF A WARRIOR WITH A DEGENERATE FEMALE

She scanned the contents, becoming more and more puzzled as she did so. The narrative contained many examples of the warrior caste capturing women of the defeated civilisation and subjecting them to various forms of humiliating experiences. In particular, one activity, which kept recurring in various variations, was for the warrior to climb on top of the woman and insert some part of his body into hers.

She read on, her mystification becoming greater.

Surely the activities described were physiologically

impossible and in the end she decided that the whole thing was some kind of allegory, with the captive women somehow standing for their conquered people as a whole. She closed the book with a snap, not bothering to replace it and removed the device from her head.

Instantly the room reappeared with Jon sitting directly opposite her, with the usual look of concern on his tired face.

'How long was I gone?' she asked hoarsely; the trips into the visualiser always left her thirsty.

'Not long,' he replied, 'perhaps a little longer than last time.'

She shook her head: time seemed to move much more quickly during her forays into that weird world.

'What did you see this time?' he said and Shana thought for a moment there was a note of envy in his voice as he handed her a tumbler of water.

She told him of the odd book about warriors and Degenerate women and the peculiar practices described therein.

'At one point it says – and I quote – "he poured his boiling seed into her." '

Jon furrowed his brow. 'That's hard to understand. Why having boiled some seed would you throw it away like that? They can't be short of food – wherever they are or were.'

Shana raised her hands high to demonstrate incomprehension and then a thought struck her. 'It says he poured the boiling seed *into* her. That would surely be painful and those people did seem to take a delight in inflicting pain.'

Jon grimaced. 'Of course. Typical of them.'

'And they had other peculiar activities as well.'

'Like what?' groaned Jon. It was hard keeping up with all the oddities than Shana kept reporting.

'I'll show you but you have to take your clothes off.'

'My clothes off? Why?'

'Trust me. I just want to see if this works.'

To Jon's surprise she had already divested herself of the

125

small amount of clothing she normally wore and was lying supine on the bed.

'What are you doing?' he said exasperatedly.

'You'll see, I'm just trying something out. Now lie on top of me.'

'What?'

'Just do it Jon and stop complaining.'

Reluctantly Jon obeyed and lay on top of Shana, his toes reaching slightly further down the bed than hers.

'Now what?'

'Move your hips up and down so you're pressing into me and then releasing.'

'And why should I do that?'

'Jon, for once in your life just do as I ask!'

Jon assumed his best put-upon expression and complied. Some moments passed.

And then a few more.

In the end he said, 'Nothing's happening. What's supposed to be happening?'

She shook her head in annoyance. 'Well, a bit more than this. This isn't how the book described it. The way they said it, it was something very exciting – for the warrior at least.'

'Obviously I'm no warrior,' Jon grunted as he removed himself from his soft human mattress and got dressed.

She did the same, shaking her head. 'There so many things that are difficult to understand. And it's so tiring when I'm in there. This last time it felt like I was in there for a whole time of light.'

'Then you won't be going in there again in this period,' Jon said.

There was no reply and turning around he discovered that Shana had got back on the bed and was now asleep.

* * *

Jon was concerned that Shana was spending too much time in the world of the visualiser for every time she returned from it she was more tired, more drained than the previous occasion. But she refused to stop.

'There are answers in there Jon, and in those answers there must be the explanation for all these things we don't understand; why the world is like it is, what is the Gate of Light and, most importantly of all, who is Korok.'

Jon was not convinced. 'But you have told me that what you see is vast. How long do you think it will take to find the answers, even if they are there?'

Shana shrugged. 'I don't know but it will take forever if I don't keep going in and we don't have forever.'

'I could just tell you not to go back in.'

Shana looked directly at him. 'Yes you could Jon. But that would not be a good idea. The only thing we have against all this madness is our trust and respect for each other. Would you really want to jeopardise that?'

He had no answer so she placed a hand on his shoulder.

'Jon, if I really think it's harming me I will stop. Trust me.'

He nodded and she gave him another quick kiss.

And she immediately put the visualiser back on her head.

She was back in the corridor of books again and she took the nearest volume off its shelf. It was heavy so she had to sit down in order to support it on her lap.

This one was entitled:

FORERUNNERS OF THE PROTECTORATE

As she leafed through it she discovered it consisted of a series of highly condensed descriptions of the thoughts and actions of many individuals whom the writer considered to be people who had contributed to the thought processes of an entity known as "The Protectorate", which was apparently the society of which the writer was a member.

Some of the people mentioned such as Machiavelli, de Sade

or Nietzsche had been mainly theoreticians or fantasists; but others such as Subutai or Timur the Lame had been men who preferred actions to theory. And what actions! Shana grew more and more revulsed, as with horror she read of cities whose entire populations had been massacred because a single stone had been thrown in its defence; elsewhere she read of how those who had dared to resist the conquerors had been killed in their thousands and their bleached skulls piled into pyramids. Once again she read of how the civilisation of the Degenerates had fallen short of these high ideals as the book closed with the mocking words: "They became more and more afraid of risk; more and more afraid of danger and tried to create a world in which danger did not exist. But in the end, danger came looking for them."

She threw the book away. She wanted no more of this "Protectorate" or its illustrious predecessors. Perhaps Jon was right: that if there were answers in here it would take far too long to find them.

She resumed her exploration of this building in which she found herself. No longer was she merely shown visions, now she was part of the vision.

And so it was she came again into the large room with the table at one end. She looked around but seemed to be alone and so she went up to the table and stopped when she was close enough to read the words upon it.

FORBIDDEN: THE BOOKS HERE ARE FOR HIGH OFFICIALS ONLY

is what she read and then she saw that on the table were two keys, one green and one red. Beyond the table there was a room which had a transparent door and she could see that the room beyond had shelves with books upon them just like the corridor she had recently traversed. She came up to the table and saw that between the keys was another piece of writing. This time it said:

"The books in this room are to be read only by High Officials. They contain works by so-called thinkers of the

128

Degenerates and are kept here to show how far from the truth the human mind can sink. They are not to be looked at by ordinary ranks."

Shana felt a thrill of hope; perhaps here she would find out more about the enemies of the Protectorate and how this bizarre world had come about. She reached for the nearest key.

And became instantly aware that two shapes had appeared on either side of her.

She turned, somehow knowing what she would see.

And she was not wrong. On either side of her stood two squat, repulsive forms with squarish heads bearing wide lipless mouths. Their eyes were unnaturally crystalline and glowed dimly with an inner ruby light. They were short, their heads coming up to just above her hips. They were not Akraz and Zarka reborn but were disquietingly similar.

'Hello Shana,' the one on the left said, looking directly up at her. The other also said 'Hello Shana' but she did not bother to turn to look at him. The first said, 'My name is…'

She put up a hand, palm facing him. 'Don't tell me your name. It will make it easier for me when I kill you.'

The creature's expression did not change, for its face did not seem to possess sufficient mobility to carry different looks. 'You may find that difficult. Perhaps you have not remembered that in here you do not have a weapon.'

Shana felt a stab of a sudden chill. Of course – she was not physically here and could not possibly have a weapon. But if she was not actually here - could she be harmed here?

'Oh yes, you can come to grief here,' the other said behind her, 'if that is what you're thinking.'

Shana walked slightly backwards so she had both of them in her view.

'And what do you want?' she asked dully.

Both creatures had now turned so they were directly facing her.

'We know what you want. You want to look at the forbidden books of the Degenerates, to wallow in their effeminate filth. But you are not a High Official.'

'And so?'

'And so you must pass a test. If you pass you can have the key to open the door to the forbidden books.'

'And if I simply go back to where I came from?'

'We will not let you go back. Try it.'

She touched the top of her head. The visualiser was not there.

'We have hidden it from you. Pass the test and we will return it.'

'And if I fail the test?'

'Then you will stay here for ever and ever and we will play together.'

Never had Shana heard the word "play" carry such sinister overtones.

'Now come up to the table, Shana.'

They pointed to the two keys and the one on the right said, 'One key opens the door to the forbidden books, the other does nothing. Well, not exactly nothing – it will open our playroom for you.'

Shana felt her fear ebb slightly and a pulse of burning anger begin to replace it.

'What is the test?' she demanded, although in truth she had already guessed it.

'For the purpose of this test, one of us always tells the truth; the other always lies. You can ask one of us one question only about which key is the correct one. After you have asked the question you will receive a reply and we will then tell you whether you will be staying to play with us.'

Shana looked into the face of the creature which was speaking. Was the mouth jerking as if attempting to form a smile?

'We do hope you'll be staying to play with us.'

Silence fell. Then the other creature spoke: 'We have completed our explanation. You must speak now and you must ask the question.'

Shana looked at the table and the two keys: one green, one red. She must not panic, she must still the whirlpool her thoughts had become.

Moments passed. The silence seemed to hang heavily over her like a suffocating cloak.

Then she had it.

She turned to the being which had spoken first and said: 'Which key would the other creature say was the correct one?'

Neither of them moved or made any signs of the beginnings of emotion. Then the one she had addressed said: 'The red key.'

Triumphantly she picked up the green one.

Both creatures suddenly made a lunge towards her. She tossed the key on the floor behind her, stepped back, softened her knees and raised her arms, adopting a fighting position.

'Is the Protectorate home to creatures who do not keep their word?' she snarled, 'I have no sword but I will take you down!'

Still they came on.

Ready to fight, she decided on a final stratagem.

'The Lord Korok will not be pleased with your cowardice.'

They stopped, turned to look at each other.

And vanished.

They did not become translucent, transparent or misty.

They just vanished.

Shana wiped her forehead and then touched her scalp. The visualiser was back.

* * *

Once again Jon found himself looking down on an unconscious Shana. She had torn the visualiser off her head and immediately fallen into a deep sleep in which she lay completely motionless except for her breathing.

He paced back and forth in the room: What if she didn't come out of it this time, if she had pushed herself too far?

It was then he heard a movement behind him and spinning around was overjoyed to see her sitting up, and not just sitting up but with a broad smile on her face!

He rushed over to her. 'Shana are you all right?'

She continued smiling and swung her feet onto the floor.

'Yes I'm alright and I won't be going back in. Jon, I've found it!'

'Found it? What are you talking about?'

She reached up and held his face between her hands. 'Jon, I found books that weren't written by the Protectorate!'

He looked puzzled.

'Jon, they were written by the people who were conquered by the Protectorate, or at least, those who inspired that civilisation.'

'Go on.'

'The names meant nothing to me but the books talked of cultures called Classical Greece, the Renaissance, the Enlightenment.'

Jon looked singularly unimpressed. 'Go on.'

'The books talked of people like Siddhartha Gautama, of Immanuel Kant and many others. Jon, I was in there for periods and periods!'

'You were not,' Jon said in annoyed tones, 'Do you think I would have let you in there that long!'

She ignored him. 'But there was one man whose writing gave me the answer!'

Jon looked sceptical but he gave her a reassuring pat on the shoulder.

'If you have it then please tell me. I'd really like to know.'

She seemed to look past him, through him as she said in an increasingly excited voice:

'There was a man called Plato who wondered long and hard about the nature of reality. He told a tale of people who were imprisoned in a cave with their backs to the entrance so all they could see was the wall in front of them. And as things happened outside the cave, as people passed by, their shadows were cast on the wall.'

'And so?'

She grasped his hand in a grip he found excessively tight.

'Jon, those people had never seen the outside world! All they had ever seen were shadows! They thought the shadows were the real world!'

He tried to remove his hand but found he could not. 'And just what has this got to do with us?'

She stood up, tall, strong, triumphant: 'Jon, we are the prisoners! We are in the cave of shadows!'

Nine

Jon and Shana walked along the village street, ignoring all the people who were studiously ignoring them.

Shana felt somewhat dispirited; after all, it is one thing to know that you are a prisoner in a cave but quite another to know that fact but not to know the location of the exit from that oubliette. As she thought over and over about their situation, she had felt exultation slowly drain out of her. Where could the exit be? Where?

Jon had been no help: she was not even sure that he believed her about the cave of shadows. Yet it had seemed so obvious when she had been reading about it; it answered so many problems, solved so many mysteries. She looked around, looking out over the edge of the hill to where the savage terrain that she had crossed to reach here lay unfolded below her like a map and then looked up at the bright green sky.

Where?

It was then a shrill, excited voice cut through her musings like a knife.

'Today is the day! Today! The time of the hunt!'

She felt Jon stiffen beside her as he came to an abrupt halt. She felt tension crackle across the air between them.

'We should go back to the house,' he said, looking around in an agitated fashion as if expecting to see something. 'And quickly.'

'Why Jon? What's the matter?'

'Something I don't want to see again,' he muttered.

They turned but found their retreat hampered by a throng of people excitedly going in the opposite direction.

'We'll wait until they've gone,' Jon growled, still looking around as if something dangerous was approaching.

But the crowd came to a halt and they found themselves trapped in a mass of chattering, gabbling people in a state of high excitement.

'Jon, what is it? Tell me!' Shana said in a quiet voice, brittle with concern.

'Something very bad,' was the only response.

Just then someone standing close yelled: 'Here it comes!'

Shana looked in the direction in which he was pointing and saw a small ball of bright blue light floating leisurely through the air towards them. Then it began to dart this way and that as if hunting for something.

'Jon what is it?' she whispered in growing alarm. The way it was now moving was horribly like a predator hunting for a small animal in the undergrowth.

'It's one of the traditions here,' Jon grated, 'when it settles on someone they're marked for death.'

'What!' Shana gasped. She spun back to follow the movements of the ball of light.

It had stopped directly above a man who immediately looked terrified and began crying out 'No! No! Not me!'

Instinctively Shana moved forward to see if she could do anything but Jon's strong grip held her fast.

'Don't move. You can't save him now.'

But then the unexpected happened. The ball did not touch the man but rose back up and began its questing again. Then its side to side movements stopped and it began a straight-line path.

Straight toward Shana.

It hovered briefly above her head and then descended, sending rippling waves of blue-white light cascading down her body. She was motionless within the curtain of light and Jon could see her wide-eyed expression of horror and her lips forming the words: 'Help me Jon!'

Immediately the cry went up: 'The Degenerate! Kill the Degenerate!'

135

The light disappeared leaving them facing a spittle-flecked crowd that was now surging forward, gripped in roaring blood lust.

Jon roared: 'Shana! To my back – now!'

She turned and stood so they were now back-to-back facing the mob. And they were not alone.

Jon had the terrible short stabbing sword of the Lords of the Sands and Shana wielded Akraz's dreadful long slashing sword. Jon's sword absorbed every scrap of light that fell on it but Shana's blazed brilliantly like captive lightning. Together they formed a whirling circle of deadly steel that few dared approach.

'Now what?' Shana gasped.

'We leave the way we came,' was the grim reply.

And so they began the long retreat back towards the house, protected by the circle of death they maintained around them. The mob followed; occasionally an individual, egged on by the others, would dare to approach the thirsty steel. Most drew back as they got near; a few did not and fell where they stood.

'Jon!' Shana panted, 'this is no good! We can't go back to the house – they'll simply surround it and burn it down!'

'We have to find a way out,' Jon said, mainly to himself.

'But where? There's nowhere to go!'

Then like a thunderclap it came to him.

'We go to the place that Korok doesn't want us to go!'

'Where? Where?' Shana cried as she lopped the arm off someone who had come too close.

'The Gate of Light. It's the only place left.'

Suddenly it was obvious to Shana too: it had to be the Gate of Light.

They changed direction, passing between the houses towards the slope that lead up to that enigmatic column of brilliance.

Suddenly Jon felt the hairs on his head and arms rise and a prickling tingle ran over his torso. Swiftly he glanced up and then

136

immediately he grasped Shana and threw the two of them to one side. One immeasurable instant later a great column of blazing blue-white heat came down, striking the exact spot on which they had been standing. The heat roared over them like the tongues of hungry beasts. And then it was gone.

Jon looked behind to see that the crowd had fallen back as the fire had come down, giving them some precious extra time. He tugged at Shana and pulled her to her feet.

'Come on before he tries again!'

They staggered on as the ground before them began to rise into a severe slope. As they climbed higher fewer people followed. Above them, the great column of light loomed larger and larger but remained completely soundless. The last scraps of vegetation died out and then, abruptly, they were nearly at the flat summit of the hill. They looked down: no-one was following - the Gate of Light was too powerful, too mysterious, too potent for any but themselves to approach.

They turned. The great column took up a good half of the summit and remained totally inscrutable. It shone in endless variations of brilliant blue, ever shifting like a sea; it was never the same shade twice and yet it always gave the feeling of being merely the surface of a blue immensity, a surface which covered depths that could not be plumbed.

They glanced at each other for a moment and then began to walk over the stony surface towards the silent structure.

It grew before their amazed eyes, becoming vaster, more gigantic, more overwhelmingly tremendous than they could have imagined. A glance upward showed it dwindling very slowly into a thin cone that had no terminus, no end, a structure that must stretch to mathematical infinity.

They were almost within touching distance. To their astounded vision the surface was as completely smooth as the finest glass and in a continual swirling, bewildering motion.

And then came the voice. A voice that shook their bones,

made their eyes roll back into their heads and by its very force and intensity made them drop to their knees.

It was a voice that could have been that of mighty slabs of rock, smashing together in a colossal avalanche.

'You will go no farther. You have angered me greatly. I had hopes for you and you have turned that hope against me. In your ingratitude, you have earned my just wrath which I will now visit upon you. I could have given you a swift death, a release from agony but you have caused me to turn even from that boon. So here is your reward.'

And with that, it started. Pain began in every part of their bodies: their fingers, their hands, their legs, their eyes. There came a host of intangible, esurient blades slicing through soft skin, slicing deeper and deeper, passing through the bone, the marrow; peeling the flesh off in thin, bloody sheets. It was pain no mind could tolerate; the only escape was into red madness.

But something started to happen. In the cores of Jon and Shana's being a small sphere of peace, of quietude, began to form. In each person it grew faster and faster, driving the agony before it and dressing the wounds with healing balm. The spheres of influence met each other and merged.

And Jon and Shana together threw off the ripping claws of the clinging pain and stood up again.

They were free and pain was just a bad dream. And then it was nothing at all.

Shana stood facing the enigmatic column and raised both her arms in triumph.

She shouted in a voice that carried strength and hard-earned authority.

'Korok! Whoever you are! Whatever you are! Jon and Shana are coming for you!'

They glanced at each other briefly, held hands briefly.

And then Jon and Shana entered the Gate of Light.

THE WORLD OF LIGHT

One

Jon felt that he was at the bottom of a vastly deep volume of black water and that it was absolutely imperative that he get to the surface as quickly as possible. But how? – he was unable to move any part of his body or even open his eyes.

It was no good trying to struggle for it was literally impossible to do so. He must be dead. This was what death was like. This was eternity.

But then he was somehow conscious of a kind of movement, a kind of upward motion. He could not explain it even to himself but it was as if he was indeed moving rapidly upward through that tremendous depth of starless blackness, up to the unknown surface.

And then he broke through that surface and was instantly aware that there was light, a harsh bluish light, burning through his eyelids. It took every atom of strength that his body possessed but he forced the eyelids open against a sticky, clinging resistance.

Light! Was there anything more beautiful, more glorious than light!

And yet he realised that there was still liquid above his eyes, a thick colourless liquid that was causing the light to streak and ripple. Panic returned but even as it did so he saw that the liquid was slowly draining away and his head was emerging into air.

After what seemed an age it had all disappeared, with just a few slowly moving drops adhering to his skin. Still all was not well; there was a sick, rubbery taste in his mouth, caused he suddenly realised by a tube that was taking up most of its volume. And his nostrils were closed firmly shut by a small clamp. He pulled the pipe out of his mouth and tried to remove the clamp from his nose but under his grasp it crumbled into tiny particles of dust.

His nostrils were almost blocked by glutinous mucus but eventually he was able to draw great draughts of air into his lungs. But the air tasted bad; it tasted of metals and artificial materials and somehow of senescence; as if the air itself was very, very old.

He tried to rise but hit his head on a transparent covering. He was in some kind of box that had various outlets in its sides into which various pipes and wires were slowly retracting. His body he noticed was covered in little indentations where presumably those implements had been attached until recently.

Once again panic returned as he realised the nature of his incarceration and he began to push desperately against the transparent covering. To his gratified surprise it immediately yielded and rose up, allowing him to step out.

He stood outside his box or casket and looked around and was astounded beyond description to see that he was in a huge room made apparently of a dull grey metal, whose walls and ceiling were both staggeringly distant. But that was not the greatest wonder: his casket was not alone; it was one of a large number that stretched in all directions.

He began to cross to the nearest and was stopped by a stab of pain from his legs. It felt as if he was attempting to push himself through thorn bushes on legs made of stone. He was forced to lean on that casket for some time until the pain in his limbs began to subside. When he eventually looked into the casket he wasn't entirely surprised to see that it contained the figure of a being very similar to himself but with many thin pipes and tubes apparently entering the body. The eyes were shut and a pipe was firmly attached to the mouth. And the somnolent body was floating in a liquid that looked much thicker than water.

Jon looked around the room trying to estimate how many of these bodies there must be but his head was too fuzzy and he gave up. Hundreds certainly.

But more importantly – he was the only one who had

emerged from its strange chrysalis: he was alone in a huge room full of comatose beings. And also, he finally realised, he was completely naked. And there was another oddity: between his legs was a bulbous sack with a fleshy tube hanging down. He touched it and could feel the touch: it was definitely an integral part of him. Most odd.

Completely at a loss as to what to do, he began to walk up and down between the caskets to see if he could determine what was the purpose of all these structures. Initially he looked into each one as he passed but soon became bored by the repetition of motionless forms floating in liquid, all completely oblivious of him, or anything else for that matter.

But as he walked he gradually realised that his movements were becoming easier; he could feel strength and suppleness very slowly returning. But as his vitality returned he also became aware that he was ravenously hungry. Ravenously hungry in a cavern of grey metal.

He leaned back against a casket and tried to remember how he had got here. Were there memories further back than just a few minutes ago? He couldn't recall any. Had he just been born, born from an artificial womb of a mechanical mother?

It was just as he had reached that dispiriting conclusion that he felt a vibration in the substance of the casket that was leaning against. He spun around to see that the liquid inside was draining away and that the pipes were pulling away from the figure inside. Fascinated he watched the person's eyelids flutter and open. The figure pulled the pipe from its mouth and began to toss its head from side to side in obvious anxiety. Jon tried to catch the person's attention but to no avail. He stood rapidly aside as the cover made a groaning vibration and then slowly rose up.

A figure stood up as the cover finished its retreat and slowly stepped out. Jon stared in amazement at what was revealed. It was something not too dissimilar from himself in that it possessed legs, arms and a head, but the body was constructed

142

entirely from curves and the head was topped with a mass of amber-gold hair, formed into a kind of cap by the residual liquid. And there was also amber-gold hair between the legs, as well as an indication of some kind of indentation in the centre.

She, for such the being obviously was, stood there blinking in the unaccustomed light, rubbing her eyes to get rid of the residual liquid. Then as she turned she saw Jon for the first time and started. Her hand flew to her side with fingers searching for something that she expected to be hanging there but was not. Then her eyes widened in joy and amazement.

'Jon!' she gasped, joy flooding her features.

* * *

'Do you remember anything?' asked the woman, whose name she had informed him earlier was "Shana", 'you must remember something!'

Jon placed his chin on the backs of his thumbs and stared moodily at the floor. She gazed at him with an odd mixture of worry and impatience. Finally he said: 'There was a hill.'

A broad smile lit up her features. 'Yes, Jon a hill! But there's much more! What about the hill?'

He waved at her to leave him alone and stood up angrily. 'A hill, a hill! What more is there to remember! And I'm hungry. How can I be expected to remember things if I'm hungry!'

Shana's smile vanished abruptly. Jon was right – she was hungry too, terribly, terribly hungry.

Jon glared at her. 'Maybe I could eat you. You seem to have plenty of spare flesh that's not doing anything.'

Shana was tempted for a moment to cover her breasts but thought better of it. She was what she was and this man had his own physical excrescences that appeared to be functionless.

It was then that their impasse was shattered as a directionless voice suddenly boomed out: 'Shana12! Jon21!

Proceed at once to the cleansing station!'

They both looked at each other in amazement. They were not alone! There was somebody else awake in this building!

Even as those thoughts flashed through their minds there was a metallic grinding noise behind them as if something that had not moved for a very long time was finally trying to do so. They spun around to see a section of the wall slowly and jerkily begin to slide open, gradually revealing a brilliantly lit corridor. Twice it stopped, making an angry whirring noise, before moving again to complete its journey.

They stared at each other for several moments before Jon said; 'Come on – if we stay here we die slowly, so nothing out there can be worse.'

They stepped out in the corridor. It was very cold with a thin film of frost clinging to the curved walls. The frost was slowly subliming, with the resultant water vapour being sucked away into vents in the wall. The temperature was rising rapidly, leading to the suspicion that not long previously the corridor had been cold: very, very cold. They stood watching the little curls of vapour vanish, not at all sure what to do. But then on the wall a glowing arrow appeared, pointing straight down the corridor before them and at its tip were the words CLEANSING ROOM. After one more glance at each other they obeyed the implicit instruction of the sign.

As they walked the temperature continued to climb until it was warm enough for their shivering to stop. After many twists and turns through the damp, grey corridors they reached a section where there were glowing words on the wall, stating: CLEANSING ROOM. They stood before it and watched with growing impatience as another section attempted to slide open, whirring and clunking as it did so. This took quite a while longer than the original door but eventually it was wide enough for them to enter.

Inside were cubicles with many vents in their walls and

fronted with transparent doors. These opened as they approached and the same commanding voice told them to enter. No sooner had they done so when the doors swung shut. Suspecting a trap, Jon had just begun to raise his fists to try and batter his way out when he was hit simultaneously by thin jets of extremely hot water which swiftly covered him in a bubbling white lather. He was rapidly covered from head to toe in the clinging foam which, in turn, was blown away by blasts of warm air. The door then opened, fortunately without any whirring or clanking, and he stepped back into the main room, feeling remarkably fresh and invigorated.

He turned just in time so see Shana step out and was pleasantly surprised by the transformation she had undergone. The globules of mucus-like liquid had vanished from her skin, which now gleamed with a rich, almost luminous, sheen, reminiscent of rosewood. And her hair had gone from a streaked, greasy cap to a tumbling, cloud-like mass of amber-gold glory.

Jon thought of saying that she looked "Good enough to eat" but decided that would be distinctly unwise under the circumstances. Instead he merely commented, 'You look better.'

She looked him up and down. 'And so do you.'

Their mutual admiration was interrupted by the directionless voice which commanded: 'Now get dressed. Clothing is on the shelves to your left.'

They found one-piece garments of a soft grey cloth that fitted them perfectly, hiding those useless excrescences. They were puzzled by two pairs of small objects with large holes on the tops before Shana realised that they were intended to go over the feet.

Now fully dressed, they looked around to see if there was anything to eat but to their great disappointment the room held a large number of cleansing cubicles and shelves but nothing edible.

'Jon we can't go on like this,' Shana said in growing

145

desperation. 'my body is tearing itself apart!'

'I know, I know,' Jon replied, 'but this place isn't trying to hurt us. There must be some food somewhere. We've just got to hold out! And' he added, giving her a severe stare, 'no more talk about hills and remembering things until we've found it!'

Two

After another futile search of the Cleansing Room, the pair returned to examining the corridor to see if it led them to somewhere more useful than a washroom.

'Jon, I can't go on much longer,' Shana whispered, 'it's not just food, my mouth is so dry I can hardly speak.'

'Then don't,' was Jon's snapped reply.

Suddenly they came upon a fork in the corridor; one passage was dark and quiet but from the other there came a buzzing noise coupled with occasional flashes of vivid blue light.

'People?' hazarded Shana.

'Let's find out,' and with that Jon began to stride down the noisy branch, towards the flashes of light.

They came around a corner and stopped in shock. Ahead of them, on the floor and on the wall, were things that looked like spiders, spiders somewhat bigger than Jon's outstretched hand and seemingly made of a flexible metal. The ones on the wall had removed a section of it and were clustered around and inside the resulting cavity. The cavity contained many pipes and cables, which were being periodically sent into high relief by the flashes, which in turn were emanating from the front legs of those spiders which were actually inside it. The spider-things on the floor were holding a curved piece of metal which could only be the missing section of the wall.

'And what are these?' Shana queried, as her shock subsided.

'They appear to be small machines that are repairing a larger machine,' observed Jon, feeling that another piece of knowledge was slowly coming into focus.

Machines. He knew about machines.

'Then we're inside a machine,' Shana concluded, 'Could we be inside some kind of vessel?'

Jon stood still and listened to his environment, both externally and proprioceptively.

There were the fierce crackles of the discharges emitted by the spider-things; the soft sound of air moving past them propelled by some distant force and coming up through his feet, his thighs, a very faint humming, a very faint rhythmic shuddering.

That was all.

He turned to Shana. 'Do you have any sense of motion?'

She considered for a moment. 'No.'

'Then we can't be moving. We must be in some very large metal building and these things are an automatic repair system.'

Her brow wrinkled for a moment, then: 'Yes. Automatic. I remember *automatic.*'

They skirted the group of toiling arachnoids which completely ignored them and went on. Their desperation was now at a pitch that they could not conceive of becoming greater.

They passed a section of wall that contained a rectangle of what appeared to be black glass. As she passed Shana noticed it flickered with a dim glow for a second and she called Jon back.

'Jon. Look at this. It might be important.'

Jon approached that part of the wall and as he got near, it flickered with a momentary flash of soft light. He stared at her but not with admiration.

'And so? Can we eat this?'

As he said so he placed one hand on that part of the wall and in his exhaustion leaned against it. Immediately there was a brilliant display of whirling kaleidoscopic colours in intricate moiré patterns. They stabilised and an image appeared.

The image of a man. A thick, heavily set man whose black jaw and scalp indicated an extremely thorough shave.

'State your requirement,' the image said in tones that indicated that immediate obedience was necessary.

The starving pair looked at each other in bafflement but

148

Shana recovered first.

'Where are we?' she asked.

The image of the man did not alter and Jon observed that the man did not appear to be blinking or moving his head, even in the slightest.

'That is not a requirement,' the image said, 'state your requirement. Otherwise this station will shut down in five seconds.'

Jon knew what his requirement was: 'Food,' he roared, 'we need food!'

The image disappeared and was replaced by a schematic that showed glowing lines which could only be representations of corridors. In one corner were two small blinking lights.

'That must be us,' Shana whispered, her breathing coming faster in her excited hope.

And Jon pointed to a large red square. 'And that must be where we need to go. Come on!'

They hurried on, encountering another group of arachnoids, which this time was investigating a hole in the floor, and came to a red door occupying the space that the schematic had indicated. In trembling excitement they rushed in, almost before the door had finished opening.

There was no food to be seen.

Jon groaned but Shana said, 'No, it's alright. They wouldn't have food permanently on display, now would they. There must be some way of getting it, of ordering it.'

Her questing gaze fell on another panel of the black glassy substance and she gave a cry of triumph.

'Ah ha! This must be it!'

She placed her palm on the panel and it immediately sprang into life, going through the usual kaleidoscopic routine before stabilising on an image of a man.

The same man who had appeared on the earlier panel.

'State your requirement,' he said.

They did.

A few minutes passed as they sat in worried anticipation.

And on the gleaming white surface in front of them, circular lids opened and there was a sudden waft of many incredible aromas and, in front of eyes which were both amazed and delighted, plates covered with varicoloured items rose up. Smaller lids slid open, revealing knives, forks and spoons.

For a moment they were simply too stunned to move and just sat there, drinking in the wonderful smells of the food and watching the little wisps of steam drift upwards.

For a horrible few seconds they feared that this was all an illusion or some devilish act of sadism, in which food would be shown to them and then whisked away as they reached for it.

They reached for it and it was still there.

But not for long. For quite some time there were no noises except the sound of masticating, swallowing, drinking, more mastication, more swallowing.

And then when every scrap of food had been consumed, every drop of drink swallowed, Jon put his hand on the screen and did it all over again.

* * *

'I remember,' said Jon slowly, as the last crumb began its journey down his gullet, 'there was a man. I think his name was Jarz.'

Shana nodded, putting down the flask of clear liquid she had been drinking from. It was her third refill.

'Yes, there was. I knew him too. But there was so much else. Who did you meet on your way to the hill, Jon?'

Jon's forehead became furrowed and his entire face twisted under the apparent huge strain of remembrance.

'The – the – the Lords.' He looked up suddenly. 'The Lords of the Sands. I had to fight them, they wanted to kill me! I still bear the …'

He looked down at his chest and pulled the fabric of his tunic out, away from the flesh. There were no scars. He leaned back in his chair – there were other memories he knew that needed to be retrieved, important memories of events that were vitally important when they had occurred; matters of life and death.

His face twisted again and again as he strove to pull up the memories out of the clinging darkness that tried to hold on to them.

'Yes Jarz was there. He told me he was my friend but in the end he was not. And there were other people, crowds of people. And light, a great pillar of light reaching up into the red sky, as far as the eye could follow.'

Shana nodded eagerly. 'Yes, I remember the great pillar of light too. It was very important to us at the time. And I remember that there were awful creatures that wanted … Ahhh!'

Jon looked sharply at Shana. 'What's the matter?'

'Nothing, nothing. Just an odd feeling down - down below. As if I'm full of something.'

'Is that all? Too much food, too quickly. Now go on – you were telling me what you recall.'

'Yes, horrible creatures that kept asking me questions and wanting to harm me. And there's another thing. Where we are now doesn't look anything like where we were. We're in some huge metal building. Did you see a huge metal building on your way to the hill?'

'No.'

'Neither did I. And we were on the top of a hill, remember. Any huge metal building should have been visible from that top. And there was noth … Ahhh!'

Jon looked at Shana with mounting concern. Her face was twisted as if in great anguish and she was squirming incessantly upon her chair.

'Shana what is it?'

She looked desperately around and her squirming became manic.

'I don't know! Jon something's trying to get out! I can't stand it!'

And with that, she leapt up and after a few more moments of looking around she dashed out of sight around a corner of the room. Shortly afterwards Jon heard the sound of water splashing onto the floor and a deep 'Ahhhhhhhhh!' from Shana. He was halfway to where he had seen her disappear when she came back around the corner, tugging her tunic and looking much more relaxed. 'That's much better!' she said, with a broad smile.

'What is?'

She sat back down and looked at him with a half-amused expression.

'Jon, I seem to recall that we had some strange doubts about the life we had before. How things didn't seem right, didn't make sense. I'm sure that on one occasion I said something to you about food and drink.'

'What – that you like it?'

'No. I'm sure I said that it was peculiar how we took things into our bodies but nothing came out.'

'That sounds vaguely familiar. Someone must have said it to me. Probably you.'

'Nothing comes out, I said. But now it does!'

'It does? But that would mean ...'

'Yes. There is. There's an opening in the lower part of my body that I didn't have before. You must have one too.'

Jon thought: the new baggy thing that he had noticed earlier with the fleshy tube. That must be something to do with Shana's discovery.

'Don't you feel something Jon, a feeling of pressure?' she asked.

He thought. There was an odd sensation developing in the

lower part of his torso, he must admit, but it was not too demanding – as yet.

'What does this all mean?' he asked finally, spreading his great hands.

Shana's face bore one of the expressions that Jon had come to recognise: the display of a growing sense of triumph; of discovery.

'Jon we are in a building that we should have seen before but didn't. We awoke from being inside caskets which we must have been in for a long time. Our bodies are similar to what we remember but are subtly different and seem more practical. You don't bear the scars that you thought you should have.'

Jon nodded reluctantly to each of her points.

'And your conclusion?'

She leaned forward so closely that some of her cloud of hair hung over him and her food-marinated breath invaded his nostrils.

'Jon the things we remember they cannot have been real. This – where we are now – this is reality!'

Three

Jon stared at his companion. 'This is reality. So what was it that you've been trying to get me to remember?'

Shana looked confused. 'I'm not sure Jon. But if I'm right, all that we experienced on the hill was – was just a dream.'

'No' said Jon flatly, 'It was not a dream. I recall what dreams are like and that was not one. In dreams there's no continuity, no cause and effect.' (A small portion of his mind noted, not for the first time, that his vocabulary seemed to be expanding.) 'In my time on the hill, which is becoming clearer to me by the minute, things happened in a regular sequence. The time of darkness followed the time of light in a definite pattern. And in any case there's one completely fatal objection to it all being a dream.'

'And that is?'

'Have you heard of a dream which was exactly shared by two people? You recall things happening to me and I recall things happening to you.'

Shana looked both puzzled and irritated at the same time.

'You're right of course. There is one way it could have been a dream, though.'

'And that is?'

She gave a wan, uncertain smile. 'That's if you are not real. If you are part of my dream.'

Jon rocked back, uncertain whether he was amused or angry. In the end, he settled on being amused. He reached over and grasped her wrist, squeezing tight.

'Are you dreaming this?'

She glared at him and eventually managed to extract her wrist.

'Alright Jon, we're not in a dream. We weren't in a dream. You're not dreaming me and I'm not dreaming you. And if I was dreaming up a man I'd have dreamt up a more agreeable one than you!'

They stared at each other for a few moments and then simultaneously burst out laughing.

The laughter soon faded however and the strange uncertainty of their current state came back to them.

Jon finally stood up and looked around.

'I think I feel the way that you did, now. It's a definite feeling of fullness. But if this is a normal part of life now there must be some better way of dealing with it than your method.'

There was and he found it eventually, just in time.

'Let's recap' he said, stretching his legs out in newly found comfort, 'we awoke inside cabinets, caskets whatever, without knowing how long we were in them. We are like we were but subtly different. Our bodies seem to make more sense than they used to – which would suggest that of the two types of experience, where we are now is more likely to be the true existence.'

(Once again he was mildly surprised by the ease with which he was able to express such abstract concepts, as if parts of his true abilities were gradually awakening.)

Shana nodded. 'Agreed. So where does that leave us?'

Jon gave a shrug. 'Absolutely nowhere.'

She stood up. 'Look, if there is an answer to all this, we're not going to find it just by feeding our faces. We've got to explore more of this building in the hope that we'll find something which will give us the answer.'

'Agreed.'

* * *

The corridors appeared to be endless and all exactly the same; nothing but grey metal curving this way or that. The only signs of "life" other than themselves were the squads of

155

arachnoids which they frequently encountered, always busily taking something apart or putting it back together again. Once Jon picked one up only to find that it twisted violently in his hands and then emitted a harsh alarm cry that caused the other arachnoids to menacingly surround him. To his great relief as soon as he put the ululating thing down it scurried off to join its fellows and they all busily got back to work.

'I won't try that again,' was his only comment.

'Jon,' Shana abruptly said, 'what if we get lost? All these corridors look the same!'

'We can't get lost,' Jon replied, 'we were lost before, remember, and that man in the glass panel told us where to go.'

Shana pointed to one just ahead of them. 'Let's try again.'

They activated the screen and wasted no time in stating their requirement, being careful to phrase their question in a way that would be accepted.

'We need to know our location,' Jon said to the image of the unblinking man.

Immediately a schematic appeared with two blinking figures shown in the centre. But this time there was lettering identifying other locations. They were gratified to see that there were several food-dispensing locations not too far away. But one location piqued Jon's interest.

'Look,' he said, placing a forefinger on the icon, '"High Official Generation Room." What can that be?'

Shana frowned. The phrase brought an unwelcome memory up from her subconscious. It was the phrase the two creatures had used when barring her way to the Forbidden Books: all she knew was that she "Was Not a High Official."

However, all further thoughts were driven away when the familiar directionless voice suddenly boomed out: 'Jon21! Shana12! Proceed directly to the Education Room!'

They looked at each other. Jon spoke first: 'The education room? What do they want to educate us in?'

Shana shook her head to demonstrate her ignorance. Jon crossed to the information panel and asked for the whereabouts of the Education Room.

'Not too far from the Generation Room,' he said on his return, 'I'd like to take a look at that first.'

Shana grasped his upper arm. 'Jon, I'm worried – the last time I heard those words is when I met those repulsive creatures, you know, the ones who keep asking me to solve riddles.'

'Well there are two of us now,' he responded, 'we may not have any swords but I can give them a puzzle of my own. How to avoid my fists.'

Shana looked unconvinced but fell in behind Jon as he strode off down the tunnel.

They hadn't gone far when a tremendous shudder shook both the floor and walls, causing their features to momentarily melt together into an indistinguishable blurring. They were thrown together by the seismic shock and stood holding each other for a while. Finally Shana asked the inevitable question: 'What was that?'

Jon shook his head. It didn't seem possible that he could have looked more worried than he had previously but somehow he managed it.

'I don't know.'

They waited to see if it would recur but after an anxious period of immobility they decided it would not and resumed their quest.

It was not long before they came to a large door in the curving metal of the corridor with the words "High Official Generation Room" emblazoned thereon in large red letters.

They stood before it, looking first at the imposing lettering and then at each other.

'One Generation Room,' Jon remarked, 'but how do we get in? And how do we generate a High Official once we are in?'

Shana looked both concerned and puzzled by that last

remark but finally realised it had been an attempt at a joke.

Looking around, she noticed an information panel not far from the door and activated it.

'We need access to the High Official Generation Room,' she stated in the most authoritative voice she could muster. The unblinking man stared at her out of the display.

'Password?' he said flatly.

Jon and Shana looked at each other. This was a new development: they hadn't needed such a thing before now. How could they guess a password out of the infinity of possibilities? Jon was already turning away when an idea came to Shana out of nowhere in a way she could not explain, then or ever.

She looked the figure in the viewer with a gaze as unblinking as his own and said in a voice of authority: 'Fatal Scimitar.'

The door opened.

It revealed a short passageway that terminated in another door. This one, however, opened as they approached. They came out into a room so vast that they could not see the far wall and which contained an uncountable number of transparent cylinders, filled with an opaque milky liquid. The cylinders stretched away like the columns of some vast underground mausoleum but four of them were detached from the others and would be the first to be encountered if people entered the room, giving the suggestion that they were more important than the others.

Jon stopped to look at the passageway they had just passed through. 'This wall appears to be solid lead and very thick solid lead. What were they trying to keep out?'

Shana had carried on into the room and was studying the transparent cylinders. The liquid within was in a constant, gentle motion, currents rising lazily to the top of the cylinder and then slowly down. There were illuminated display panels in front of each one showing a list of compounds with percentages next to them.

'Iron, calcium, phosphate, adenine, guanine – Jon, do you know what these are?'

Jon crossed to her and looked down at the scrolling list. 'No idea. Could be a recipe for a nice stew for all I know.'

Just then he felt something brush his thigh and turned around to see a squat metal object with multiple arms had come up to him without him noticing. It had basically a disc shaped body on segmented legs and from the disc a selection of appendages was protruding, some jointed and thick, some jointed and thin and two extremely flexible ones, like tentacles. It also had two red eyespots with which it was studying them.

'You are too close to the Generation Tubes,' it said in a high-pitched, emotionless voice, 'you may not approach within two metres.'

Jon studied the various appendages which had now been raised to the level of his crotch and decided not to argue. 'Of course,' he said and moved away. It was then he saw that the entire room was filled with at least a dozen of these mechanical things.

'What are they?' Shana whispered as she joined him.

'They seem to be a higher grade of arachnoid, which suggest they have a more important job to do.' He turned back to look at the cylinders with their gently stirring contents. 'Look there's something written on them.'

Shana scanned them from left to right, reading out the words that she saw: 'Rocha. Maroun. Gang Jianguo and … and …' Her voice faltered.

'And?'

Shana turned to Jon, her eyes wide and staring: 'The last word Jon! It's Korok! Korok!'

* * *

They were back out in the endless greyness of the endless
159

corridors.

'He's here! Somewhere in this building!' Shana said, feeling the first tendrils of hysteria beginning to invade her mind.

'Stop it!,' Jon snapped, 'we don't know that! All we saw was a name, just a name!'

She calmed herself and stared directly at him, blue-grey eyes holding Jon's brown in a steady grasp.

'In our previous existence – whatever that was – he was just a name, a curse, a figure of speech. But if this is reality and we are real beings in it – then so is Korok. And where else would he be but here?'

Jon grasped her shoulders in a grip of steel and looked deeply into her eyes. 'Shana stop thinking of Korok as some kind of demon, some kind of god. If he's a man he can bleed, if he can bleed he can die. And if he can die I will be the one who kills him.'

'You promise?' said Shana, feeling – to her amazement – the beginnings of tears at the back of her eyes.

Jon stared at Shana and had the sudden feeling that whatever it took he would save this woman from whatever threatened her, even if he had to rip up the universe to do it. But despite that sudden blast of emotion he was still absolutely unsure of what to do next and said so.

'We will go to the Education Room,' was Shana's reply.

'Why?'

'Because at the moment we're helpless little creatures scurrying around a big building, knowing nothing about where we are or what we're supposed to be doing. If that place lives up to its name it should provide us with some answers.'

Jon looked unconvinced but Shana pressed her case. 'Look Jon, remember how much I learned when I was wearing that cap thing on the hill. How I learned about the Cave of Shadows. If I hadn't gone in we'd still be there or maybe slaughtered by – by Korok.'

160

Jon finally agreed and having checked its location on another schematic set out for it. They passed several bands of toiling arachnoids who as usual totally ignored them. The second one appeared to be dealing with a particularly bad problem insofar as huge showers of blue and yellow sparks were issuing from a rip in a wall along with crackling bolts of electrical energy. It looked so dangerous that the pair were forced to find another way.

But find it they did and gained access to the room without further trouble. The Educator Room was comprised of an antechamber which had an open door in its far wall. Through this could be glimpsed a much larger room. Shana wanted to go straight through to that part of the room but Jon advised caution.

'Let's see what's in here first,' he said.

The answer was, apparently, not a lot. There was a continuous bench running three-quarters of the way around the room on which sat devices which would have reminded the pair of old-fashioned TV sets, if they had ever seen one. In front of each device was a chair. And that was all.

Jon sat on one of the chairs and inspected his immediate surroundings. He noticed a red button on the shelf in front of the device, which from its design must have been some kind of viewer and pressed it. Immediately a portion of the bench swung up revealing a vertically stacked collection of thin sheets of metal. Jon took one out: it was indeed metal and extremely thin so it bent like paper as he held it by one corner. He studied it intently and thought he could just make out extremely small marks upon its glistening surface. But they were far too small for him to be able to determine what they were.

He put the sheet back in its drawer and stood up.

'Whatever they are, they're no use to us,' he decided, 'let's see what's in the main room.'

Inside the larger room, they were confronted with row after row of long couches, at one end of which was a device that looked strangely familiar. Shana picked one up.

'Look Jon, it's like the device in your house.'

Jon studied it. Indeed it was similar to the object from his time on the Hill, possessing a curved section that terminated in two soft pads as before; but the material it was made from looked much more impressive.

'So what do we do?' he asked Shana.

'I think it's pretty obvious,' was the reply, 'we lie on the couches and put these things on our heads.'

Jon looked around at the huge number of empty couches that completely filled the entire room. 'It looks like we are the first to arrive. The others will be late for the party.'

'We already knew we were the first,' Shana said, 'stop delaying and just do it.'

She was already lying on the couch and Jon watched apprehensively as she put the headset on top of her riotous mass of hair. Instantly her eyes closed and her face went blank. Alarmed, Jon crossed to her and shook her as gently as he could but there was no response.

He stood over her for quite a while wondering what he should do. Eventually, he decided that trying to pull her out of whatever state she was in was too dangerous. There was only one way he could watch over her and that was to join her.

He lay down on the couch and very slowly placed the headset on his head. Instantly he felt tiny pinpricks as extremely small wires shot out of the ends and sank a short distance into his flesh. There was a short pang of pain and then no sensation at all.

He felt his eyes shut involuntarily.

And then his education began.

Four

There was only blackness; a blackness so deep it was if the entire universe had been annihilated. A blackness that was the negation of everything that had ever been, was or ever would be. Jon could have been hanging motionless in a universe of eternal night.

And then at what could have been any distance whatsoever he saw some spinning shapes, each glowing with soft pastel light. And slowly they began to approach him, one after the other in a short train of mystery.

Jon could see that they were regular shapes but as yet he did not possess the terminology to define them. They were, in fact, the Platonic Solids, each softly glowing with pleasing radiance except the last, the icosahedron, which was not self-radiant but a lightless, lifeless black.

The first in the line, the tetrahedron, slowly approached him until it became obvious that they would touch. And touch they did and more; Jon passed without resistance into the exact centre of the object and was immersed in its lambent substance.

And then it began.

He felt a sudden probing of his mind, as if every neuron was being studied for its contents and its holding capacity for information.

It appeared that a decision had been made because then came a vast flux of data deep into every one of those neurons; a great irresistible tidal wave of information, of concepts, of axioms, of rules of inference, as entire slabs of mathematical knowledge crashed into his brain.

He felt like screaming, of begging whatever force was responsible to stop, of pleading for respite. But still it surged on.

Then it was over and he was free, outside the tetrahedron and adrift in emptiness again.

But not for long.

The softly glowing cube approached, touched him, swallowed him.

And it began again. This time the mighty cascades were of advanced theoretical physics: special relativity, general relativity, quantum chromodynamics, non-abelian string theory. And there was practical physics also, mainly to do with rocket propulsion, but with a sinister subsection on weaponry.

And then the cube moved on.

Jon watched the glowing octahedron approach with the certainty that it too would be forcing yet more knowledge into his burning brain. And so it proved, this time of chemistry; mainly organic but with a heavy dose of planetology. And once again a disturbing area, this time on the use of chemistry for explosives.

The octahedron passed into unplumbed blackness and he was swallowed by the oncoming dodecahedron, which poured biochemical knowledge into his tottering mental circuitry.

He was released and waited for the final chapter of his ordeal by knowledge - but No! the icosahedron was dark and aloof. It passed him by without any recognition of his existence.

Jon watched it disappear into ebon oblivion and reflected that whatever knowledge it contained was not regarded as being for the likes of him.

Suddenly he realised that he was en rapport with Shana although he could not see her; he was somehow able to observe her thoughts, thoughts which were in a mind that was in total turmoil from having tremendous amounts of information poured into it. Then with what seemed like an audible snap, contact was lost. Jon hoped that was because she had come out of the Educator before him.

He then expected to awake from whatever this state was and find himself on the couch but once again he was surprised.

Now he was to be given a history lesson.

164

A great face appeared in the darkness, covering an area several times greater than Jon's dimensions. It was the face of a man whose visage bore the unmistakeable lines of power and great authority. A face seemingly not made of soft flesh but skilfully carved from dark flint. A face that was that of someone used to deciding on matters of life and death without a second's thought. A face of a man whose enmity was something to be greatly feared.

The face spoke.

'I am Maroun,' it said, in a voice that thundered through Jon's mind, 'I will show you the fate of the Degenerates and how we built the Protectorate on foundations made from their soft corpses.'

Like Shana before him, but in much greater detail, he saw in his mind scenes of past events.

He saw the gentle, peaceful cultures of the Degenerates in their last days. He saw their pathetic attempts to remove all danger from their meaningless lives; how they shrank from pain; their gnawing fear of death. He saw the people, apparently happy but in reality assailed by a million doubts, going about their myriad activities, unaware of the approach of the fatal scimitar. He saw their violent overthrow by forces both internal and external; saw their populations enslaved and brutalised.

Maroun spoke again: 'And so was formed the Protectorate; so-called because we exist to preserve all that is proud, strong and manly in humanity. People who obey orders without concern for their own safety; people prepared to leap into the furnace in the service of the Great Khan.'

Jon felt a tremendous need to speak out against this interpretation of history but he realised that would be extremely unwise. All he could do was hope that Maroun, whoever he was, could not read his thoughts.

'Now behold our army!' the voice thundered, 'let inferior breeds throughout the universe tremble at their approach!'

165

The visions changed again, this time into something Jon could recognise because he had been there not long previously. It was the room with the pods and somehow he could clearly see inside each one. At once he noticed that he was seeing the same features again and again and he soon realised that there were only ten male types (of which he was obviously one) and fifteen female types. Again and again he saw Shana's face in casket after casket.

With his new knowledge, the explanation was obvious.

'Clones!' he said to himself.

To his surprise Maroun answered him. 'Yes. But not just clones, clones made in the laboratories of the Protectorate. Clones composed of proteins utilising amino acids not found in nature; genetic material using artificial bases; all designed so that the creature composed of these substances will be stronger and longer lasting. Add blind loyalty to that robust frame and you have the perfect soldier.'

But something has gone wrong with your plan, Jon thought in the secret places of his mind, *for I do not possess blind loyalty to the Protectorate.*

As Jon studied the comatose individuals in the caskets he became aware of something else: he could sense their mentalities. In some, he could see a little bubble of awareness slowly rising in a dark column of unconsciousness. This was obviously the true meaning of the Gate of Light: it was simply the awakening of the individual from this form of stasis – just as he and Shana had done not long ago. This was what Jarz had meant when he had said that soon they would have enough arrivals to enter the Gate of Light en masse.

He decided to risk a question.

'When I was – unconscious - I thought I was in a forest surrounded by dangerous animals. Then I met strange creatures that wanted to kill me. Was that all a dream?'

'Not exactly a dream. You and all the other warriors were

166

embedded in a digital simulation of an environment that we had designed. Your individual minds were linked so that you could interact with each other. What one saw, the others saw. The simulation was not perfect due to the extremely large number of variables but it was basically consistent.'

Basically consistent, Jon thought, *just a few errors like Shana's green sky and my red one.*

'And why was it necessary to put us in that simulation?'

'Your brains could not be shut down completely whilst you were in stasis. They would have slowly decayed. Therefore we provided them with a minimum amount of stimulation to keep them healthy. And we set challenges to eliminate any soldiers who were not adequate for our purposes.'

Akraz and Zarka. The Lords of the Sands thought Jon. While Maroun had been speaking he had discovered that he was now fully immersed in the strange environment and now understood what it was. Somehow he was linked into a kind of neural net that included the minds of the people who were still in stasis; a hangover no doubt from the time when they had thought they were all on the Hill. And he was also aware that there were files of records which showed the detailed actions of the Protectorate from the time of these "synthetic humans" (what other description could there be?) up to this exact moment. Just as Shana had proved to be a natural adept on the hill in this virtual world it seemed that he possessed similar abilities in this true, master version of that system. If only he had more time...

'Soon all the warriors will be awake and we can begin new conquests,' the dread voice continued, 'but you have now learned all you need to know to be an effective soldier. You will be called when you need the Educator again.'

And this time it did end. Once again there appeared to be an audible *snap!* inside his head and his eyes opened under their own volition and he saw Shana looking down on him with concern written on her features.

167

'At last!' she said, 'I thought you were going to stay in there forever.'

'No such luck for you,' he grinned and tried to rise from the couch.

And collapsed on the floor. Instantly it was as if someone had driven a rapier through his head. As he tried to rise his vision was suddenly filled with dancing blue and yellow zig-zag lines, overlaying an abstract pattern of squares within squares within squares. With his new knowledge, he realised that he was having a migraine. A very bad migraine.

Shana helped him back onto the couch.

'It will pass soon,' she said, running soothing fingers over his temples, 'I had it too. It will pass.'

His eyes had been shut but that only made the zig-zag lines even more vivid. He opened them again and looked at Shana, trying to ignore the visual disturbances that overlaid her.

'Shana,' he finally whispered through his pain, 'I saw so much! Learned so much! And I could see your mind! Read your thoughts! It was incredible, frighteningly incredible!'

She nodded. 'I felt your mind come into – well, come into view I suppose you'd call it. I could see all the information pouring into you. And,' she concluded, somewhat bitterly, 'you were getting a lot more than me. It seems that the Protectorate doesn't want its women warriors knowing too much.'

Jon gave a weak smile, trying to ignore the fact that Shana's face was now embedded in an infinite series of ever-decreasing rectangles. 'That fits in with their world view, I guess. I saw what you had seen and much more I think. I saw the overthrow of the people they call the Degenerates and their state of oppression. The Protectorate is a terrible threat. And it seems its lust for conquest is far from satisfied. We are meant to be its new shock troopers.'

She nodded again. 'Yes, I know what we are. We are synthetic humans, built from improved versions of proteins and

168

genetic materials. Meant to wear out much more slowly so we'll be as useful as possible to the Great Khan.'

'Now we know why things seemed wrong before; all those little details that didn't make sense. All because the simulation was not perfect. And it didn't need to be, of course – because we had no life before the simulation. All the things make sense now, like – like your hole...'

Shana smiled, a smile that was subtly different from those he had seen before. 'No need to be coy, Jon. I know what my new holes are for. Just as I know what your new appendage is for. Maybe we'll try a practical lesson one day instead of all this theory. We might even have better luck than we had the last time, we certainly couldn't do any worse.'

Jon was so taken aback that for a moment he failed to realise that the visual disturbances had ended and he was now the possessor of a mere headache.

She pulled him upright. 'There, there. The worst should be over now. '

He nodded and gingerly placed his feet on the floor.

'Yes, I'm alright now. I think we need to eat again after all that.'

She shook her head. 'Not yet. We will need to eat but we need something else first.'

'And that is?'

She climbed back onto the couch, lay on her back and closed her eyes.

'Sleep.'

And they did.

* * *

Jon did not know how long they had slept; they were in an environment in which there was no way of measuring the passage of time. The Education Room looked exactly the same

169

as it had before. The only difference was internal; his hunger was even more urgent now than it had been before sleep.

He roused Shana and they went back to the food dispensing room which was as generous and accommodating as they remembered. When they could eat and drink no more he turned to his companion and said, 'We now know most of what was hidden before.'

'Most,' she replied, 'there are still mysteries.'

'Yes, of course,' he replied, somewhat irritatedly, 'but we have to deal with what we do know. And there is something very big about to happen.'

She waited.

After a tension-filled pause, he continued. 'Jarz said that soon the army would enter the Gate of Light. We now know that was just the simulation's metaphor for awakening from stasis. But it means that all the bodies in the caskets will soon be awakening and awakening as fanatical warriors of the Protectorate. But there is something different about you and me. Something happened to us which gave us independent thought, so we were never just loyal clones of the Protectorate.'

'In which case our time of freedom will be coming to a very premature end,' Shana said and gave a shrug of resigned acceptance.

'There is a possible way that we can prevent that happening.'

'And that is…'

Jon leaned forward with a strange light in his eyes. 'Remember when we were in the Educator we could look into minds. I could see your mind but more importantly, I could look into the sleeping minds of the people in the Stasis Room. If we can get into those minds before they wake, perhaps we can influence them to have independent thought.'

'And how will we do that?'

Jon's smile became grim and resolute. 'They gave me huge amounts of knowledge. Knowledge only to be used in the

170

unthinking service of those monsters. It was never intended for beings of independent thought. But I am independent.'

He stood up and pulled Shana to her feet.

'And I will use it.'

Five

Concern was written all over Shana's face as she stood before Jon. 'If you go back in you'll be at the mercy of that Maroun-thing. You can't risk it!'

'No other way,' Jon replied, 'I'm not telepathic. The only way I can influence the other minds is through the Educator which connects us into some kind of neural network. And what's the alternative? If we wait for them to wake up under their own volition they'll be fanatical Protectorate supporters. And that will be the end of us.'

Shana was silent for a while and then nodded. 'Alright.'

He grasped her shoulders and pulled her near. 'That's not all. You have to come in with me.'

He saw the alarm come into her eyes. 'Why Jon?'

'I have to know what the differences are. I have to compare a mind that is not enslaved to the Protectorate with one which is. I can't read your mind without the Educator.'

She stared at him for a few moments longer and then said: 'Let's do it.'

'When we're in, you have to think about the Protectorate and the Degenerates. And Korok. I have to see which areas light up.'

He saw her flinch slightly at the mention of the dread name but she nodded again.

Shortly they were both back in the almost tangible blackness of the Educator. This time there were no revolving polyhedra. Only the darkness.

And something else. The incorporeal nearness of another mind. Shana's.

Jon – I can see your thoughts! came a thought into his mind; a thought that was not his.

Good. Now do as I said: think about the Protectorate. Maroun. Korok.

He was aware of her distaste as he sent the instructions. He searched in the darkness for a visualisation of that thinking brain – and found it.

He saw schematics of the amygdala, the claustrum, the hippocampus. In glowing lines in the darkness.

But he saw more. He saw consciousness itself as minute transient fluctuations in the entangled quantum states at the very molecular level.

He watched the changes as the mind which rested upon this delicate substructure intoned the hated names and concepts to itself.

Far down in his own mind he embedded the images of what he had seen into his deepest memory and then thrust his straining mentality up, up through the entangled states, through the organic molecules, through the brain structures, to the uppermost level.

Now! he sent to Shana *Do the same with me!*

He set his mind to thinking about what he had seen; the callous overthrow of a peace-loving culture; the reduction of an entire people to servitude and worse.

Do you see it! He sent to Shana *Do you see the structures firing?*

There was no reply for some time and then Shana's thought came to him, thin and despairing. *Jon – I can't do it! I can't see you!*

He groaned in the fastness of his mind. He had feared that Shana did not have the talent and it had turned out as he had feared. He alone would have to carry out the task.

Do what you can he sent *See if you can find out more about where we are and why we're here!*

And with that, he disengaged his rapport with Shana and sent it into the Stasis Room.

His mentality hovered intangibly over the sleeping minds of the occupants of the caskets. He saw in which ones the rising

173

bubble of awareness was closest to breaking the surface of unconsciousness and sent his own mind into the sleeping brain.

He found the flickering entanglements of thought and saw the unmistakeable signs of rigid control by an outside force. He reached in and tried to remove those mental fetters but found they were deeply embedded in the very substance of that brain and resisted his efforts to wrench them away. Still he struggled until with a sudden release of tension he had pulled them away and watched them disintegrate.

He knew then that the release of the hundreds of minds in this room was far beyond his abilities. At most he could free ten individuals before exhaustion overtook him.

As it transpired, that was an over-optimistic estimate. He succeeded in freeing three males and two females. His last success was a female and as he pulled away he realised that this individual was one of the Shana clones! His mental vision was confined to the image the person had of him or herself: he had no direct experience of their outward shape. But the image held in the last female's brain was unambiguous – the female was identical to Shana!

He had known this was possible from his experiences on the hill of course;

But Shana had said she could distinguish between Jon11 and Jon21. He hoped that when he met this woman he would be able to tell her and Shana apart; the thought of two identical Shanas was deeply disturbing.

Exhausted beyond the possibility of further action he withdrew the tendrils of his questing mind from the female's container and searched in the velvet darkness for "his" Shana's mentality.

He found it but in a deeply troubled state.

Shana have you found anything out?

Yes came the flat response.

Then let's get out and you can tell me.

174

How do we do that?

That stopped Jon. At the end of their previous immersion, the Maroun avatar had ejected them when their lessons had been completed. How did they eject themselves?

He sent his mind out into the Education Room, searching, searching.

There was only one way.

Shana he transmitted *Visualise yourself taking off the headset. Visualise yourself getting off the couch and standing up.*

I'll try.

Jon did as he had instructed Shana. He could not see his body directly but he poured all his strength into the visualisation that he had described.

And he found his eyes had opened and he was able to take off the headset. He leapt up to see if Shana had joined him.

She had not. She was still lying completely motionless on the couch, face completely blank, eyes shut tight. She could not get out.

Jon found his heart hammering as he removed the headset. What if her mentality was forever trapped in the strange world of the Educator and her body no more than an empty structure that its occupant was now barred from?

She lay still for some time and then her eyelids fluttered and she very slowly raised herself into a sitting position. Her hair cascaded over her face, hiding her frightened expression. Eventually she turned to him. 'Jon I'm not going back into that horrible place. I couldn't get out! I was trapped in darkness!'

He held her close and nuzzled her hair.

'No you won't go back in. I've done all I could in there. I don't know if I achieved anything. We'll just have to wait. But did you discover anything, something that can help us?'

She nodded.

'What did you find out?'

'I can't speak at the moment, Jon, my whole body is shaking.

I have to sleep.'

And with that Jon felt her go limp in his grasp. She was asleep.

* * *

Shana lay there for a long time and Jon himself fell asleep after a period of watching her to see when she came back to him. When he finally regained consciousness, as usual he had no idea how much time had passed but by the stiffness of his limbs he surmised it had not been a short period. He stood up and looked down on Shana, her still face framed in an expanse of amber-gold hair. Once again he felt that stirring of emotions that he had so little experience of; a desire to pull her up from the couch and press his lips on hers. From the Educator he knew what lay behind those feelings but that did not in any way diminish the strength of his desire to do all he could for this woman; to protect from the horrors that circled them.

Finally, she stirred and he saw her gaze dart from corner to corner of the room.

'It's alright,' he said, at once bending down to be as close as possible to her, 'you're out. And you don't have to go back in.'

She sat on the edge of the couch and buried her face in her hands, her hair forming an impenetrable tent around her profile.

'The darkness. Trapped. Horrible. Horrible.'

He sat by her, an arm around her, not daring to speak, to ask questions.

After an achingly long time she raised her head and, sweeping her hair back, looked at him.

'Yes, Jon. I know you've been waiting for answers. And I have them.'

A voice behind Jon suddenly said: 'That's good. Because we'd like some answers as well.'

Jon spun around. There were five figures standing in the

doorway: three males and two females. And one of the females was Shana. He heard an intake of breath from the Shana at his side. He stood up.

'And you are?'

The first man approached. He was of a category that Jon was not familiar with.

'I'm Jorl38.'

The others followed.

'I'm Jarm40.'

'I'm Shev16'

'I'm Jarz51'

'I'm Shana36.'

Jon felt his companion rise from the couch behind him and stand at his side. In utter amazement they stared at the newcomers. Two of the males and one of the females were of types that they had only seen from a distance in the Hill simulation. But the last man looked exactly like their nemesis from that period.

And the woman was – Shana.

Jon could not help looking from the one to the other. His fears were realised – he could not tell them apart. All the newcomers were dressed exactly as he and Shana were.

He felt a crazy compulsion to put them side by side and examine them closely but that was out of the question. At least it was until "his" Shana did exactly that.

She crossed to the newcomer and looked her up and down.

'You look a bit like me,' she said quietly.

Shana36 gave an arch smile and said in an identical voice. 'I look *exactly* like you.'

To his gathering horror, Jon realised that was absolutely true. There were none of the subtle differences which had distinguished him and Jon11. It struck him that if he were to leave the room and come back in he would not be able to tell them apart.

He decided to take control of the situation. 'You've eaten I take it?' he said wondering why his first question had been such a banal one.

Jorl38 sat himself down on a couch with an assured air.

'We have. We've also been told to report to this room to be – what's the word – "educated." '

Jon stared at them. He knew he had been in rapport with five individuals in the Stasis Room and that the last one had looked like Shana. Were these the same individuals or was this a trick?

'Good,' he said, 'the Protectorate need soldiers who know one end of a gun from the other.'

Instantly the newcomers stiffened; Jarz51 looked at Shev16 and then they all turned and glared aggressively at him.

Jon waved a hand. 'It's fine; just a quick test. Relax. And Shana36...'

'Yes Jon?'

He tried to smile but was not at all sure what shape his lips were making and finally said, in a strangely strangulated voice, 'I wonder if you wouldn't mind staying on that side of the room.'

The lady in question looked at him with an expression that could only be described as *amused tolerance*.

'What's the matter, Jon – afraid you might kiss the wrong girl?'

Jon found himself unable to reply but was saved by Jorl38 who, looking at Shana12, said, 'This little lady was about to tell us something.'

She looked at Jon who nodded, 'Don't worry. Just tell us.' He glanced at the newcomers. 'You haven't been in the Educator yet so no doubt all of what she's going to say will be a great shock to you. So make sure you're all seated.'

He did not know then that it would be a great shock to him also.

Shana12 stared at them and said in crisp tones: 'Do you

178

know what you are?'

'No, tell us.'

'You are bioengineered structures created in the image of *homo sapiens* but made of less perishable materials and with a nervous system that is much better organised. You are made in the image of humanity but you are not of that genus; you are – what shall we call it? – *transhuman.*'

'Sounds good,' Jarm40 said, with a sidelong glance at Shev16.

'We have all been embedded in a simulation whilst actually residing in stasis pods for a long period of time.'

'Well, we guessed that.'

'Do you have any idea how long?'

'No.'

'Five hundred years.'

The room burst into a tumult of voices, with everyone speaking at once, repeating the same astounding phrase over and over again.

Shana12 waved them to be quiet.

'And do you know where you are?'

'Obviously not.'

Shana12 looked at Jon and for a moment he seemed to be falling deeply into bottomless pools of blue-grey mystery.

'You are passengers on the interstellar ramjet *Fatal Scimitar.*'

Six

In an environment that was nothing other than improbability piled high on improbability the information supplied by Shana did not seem to be too incredible. The other six accepted the truth of their situation after only a short delay. The newcomers then went into the Educator and met Maroun, received their upgrades and saw the sad fate of the Degenerates spread out before them. Once again the females received only a truncated version of the syllabus. On their return, Jon decided that now he had reinforcements he would make another attempt at freeing the sleepers in the Stasis Room.

But first he wanted more information. Although he accepted his Shana's revelations he wanted to know more: what was the purpose of this extraordinary journey that they had discovered that they were experiencing?

The new Shana and Shev agreed to go back into the dark world of the Educator in order to do just that. His Shana refused to contemplate it and he accepted her decision.

They donned the headsets and at once their eyes closed and their faces went blank.

Time passed. The others stared helplessly at each other and Jarz took to walking back and forth like a caged animal.

Jon had tried talking to him and was relieved to find that he was nothing like his equivalent on the Hill. But now the man was too wound up for conversation and waved at Jon to be quite when he attempted to talk. Jarm and Jorl too were plunged into quiet melancholy; Jarm spent most of the time studying his hands while Jorl, having lost some of his confident air, sat in silent immobility. Jon found himself in a peculiar state of confusion as he was in the same room as two identical Shanas, one awake and staring at him with wide-open, worried eyes; the other deeply asleep on her couch. *How long before I lose track of who's who?* he wondered.

Eventually, after what seemed an eternity, the two women's eyes fluttered and, after a few moments of confusion, the ashen-faced women looked around, removed their headsets and sat up in a slow, jerking fashion.

The room burst into activity immediately as the men crowded around the two women. Jon commanded them to be quiet and said: 'Let them rest for a while. It's not easy to do what they've done. You should know that.'

Eventually Shev, a small woman with raven black hair, said: 'I think we've found out all you wanted us to, Jon.'

'And that is?'

Shev looked at the faces of her audience, one by one and began her speech: 'What Shana12 said is true. Five hundred years ago the Protectorate launched this craft, the *Fatal Scimitar* on a journey to a nearby star.'

'And why would they do that?' demanded Jon.

Shev looked confused. 'I don't understand their mentality but it seems they believed that the planetary system of that star held an intelligent lifeform with its own civilisation.'

'And why would they make this journey?' Jorl interjected, 'to exchange gifts and give each other a big kiss?'

'No. The Protectorate needs other cultures for one purpose only – to battle and conquer. And after this new world had been conquered a new Protectorate would arise. And then they could fight that.'

'What – their own descendants!'

Shev buried her face in her hands.' Yes! yes! They would do that! They believe that only conflict justifies existence. Without enemies there is no point in living!'

'And where do Korok and this Maroun character fit in?' Jon demanded, conscious that he was perhaps pushing this frightened woman too hard.

'Maroun and others were part of an elite group of powerful men. They gave Korok the job of launching this starship. That's all I know!'

Shana36 patted her on the shoulder and took over the explanation.

'The Protectorate decided to launch an expeditionary force to this star just as – as my – uhh – sister Shana said. And it was five hundred years ago, give or take a few years. We were their chosen warriors who would do the preliminary work of subjugating the native people, if there were any, and then begin terraforming the planet.'

'And we were in stasis for all of that five hundred years?' Jon asked.

'Indeed we were. The simulation gave us just enough stimuli to keep our brains ticking over, for in truth we were all a few microns away from death, given that our metabolisms were so low. But those stimuli were on the simulation's time which was much slower than real-time. So all the events we experienced, our struggles to get to the Hill, our lives on the Hill, they seemed like a few months' worth of time to us but in reality ...'

'It was five hundred years,' Jon finished for her.

'Yes, but not quite. About two hundred years after launch this vessel passed into a void in the interstellar medium which greatly increased the cosmic ray flux hitting it. Many more high energy particles than allowed for penetrated the hull and disrupted the systems. The records don't show what I'm about to say but I think it's a likely conclusion.

'The cosmic ray flux must have affected a few individuals in the stasis pods and somehow removed the Protectorate's conditioning. You said you both went through a period when you began to doubt the reality of your surroundings. That would have been sometime after the cosmic ray burst.'

Jon turned to his Shana. 'So the Lords of the Sands, Akraz and Zarka, the troubles on the Hill. All those events played out

182

over three hundred years or so in real-time. Between one of our thoughts and the next this vessel was plunging through huge stretches of empty space. After each one of our thoughts was a day, a week – a month. Who knows?'

The incredible revelation threw a blanket of silence over all of them. They envisaged those rows of stasis pods, each containing a life; each brain holding a little flicker of thought, guttering back and forth on the edge of oblivion as the great vessel that held them like bacteria in its metal gut, plunged endlessly on through kilometre after kilometre of empty blackness.

Finally, Jon turned back to Shev; doubtingly; questioningly. 'But five hundred years? Why such an incredible time?'

Shev had recovered somewhat and raised her pinched, drawn face to look at her companions.

'The ship is moving at a large percentage of lightspeed but not a relativistic percentage. That's why we were in stasis in the first place. It's the only way biological beings such as we could make such a journey as this.'

'A war fought over these vast distances and times would hardly be that fast moving.'

Shana36 shrugged. 'The Protectorate believes that it is the final state of mankind, that its rulers will be the dispensers of life and death for the rest of human history. They are in this for the long run. No, make that – forever!'

Jorl suddenly broke into the conversation. 'Hey! Let's look on the bright side. Surely the journey must be nearly over! We'll be able to get out, stretch our legs, sample the local cuisine, visit a wine cellar or two!'

Jon looked at Shev and Shana36, reflecting as he did so that Jorl's experiences in the simulation appeared to be quite different from his. However, nothing in Jorl's words had lightened their mood.

'Isn't what Jorl said true?' he asked the pair. 'Minus the wine cellars.'

Shev gave a wan smile. 'Yes, I think the journey is nearly over. But from what I read in there it wasn't just the conditioning of a few individuals that the cosmic ray burst wrecked – it was also the guidance mechanisms of this ship. We're out of control.'

* * *

"Out of control."

Had those few words sealed all their fates, Jon wondered.

Only a short while ago they had thought themselves reasonably safe in some large building somewhere in a normal reality. But the truth was they were inside some structure of unknown dimensions and properties that was hurtling through interstellar space to some distant star system. Did fate have any more cruel tricks to play? he wondered; trying to push the black tide of despair back down into his subconscious.

But one thing was certain. Surely seven people would not be enough to change the situation in any meaningful way. If they had any chance of saving themselves they would have to have more allies. They would have to go back into the Educator.

He decided that he had to give the women a recuperation period and not ask them to accompany him; besides, they might suffer from the same problem as his Shana and not be able to get into others' minds.

He told the men what was needed and immediately Jarm said that he couldn't do it. Jon did not argue: the last thing he wanted was someone panicking in the depths of the Educator. The other two accepted his plan, though with obvious reluctance and equally obvious grim expressions.

He crossed to what he hoped was the original Shana and hugged her. 'Here we go again.'

She responded by giving him his first kiss in the real world.

It was better than he had imagined it to be in the cave of

184

shadows.

Soon the three men were in the almost palpable blackness of the Educator. Once again there were no softly glowing polyhedra: it appeared that the time for their second lesson was not nigh.

They visualised the Stasis Room and they found themselves looking at the Educator's schematic representation. Like the ghosts of mythology, their minds hovered above the pods and their comatose inhabitants.

Jon sent a thought into the network: *Get ready – On my comm...'*

But his thought was cut short by an urgent message from Jarz.

Jon – we're not alone! Someone else is in here with us!

Jon sent his mental probes in all directions as that message's import became clear.

Then he felt it.

It was as if swimmers some distance from the shore had felt something immense and powerful pass not far beneath their dangling feet.

This was not another one of his band. This was not Jarm or Shev.

The identity of the intruder was not long hidden.

In the darkness a great face appeared, much larger than Maroun's had been.

It was the strong face of a heavy-boned man with a firm powerful jaw, heavy brow ridges and eyes that projected a chilling radiance.

And then the face smiled.

A smile that was the quintessence of pure terror.

They heard his voice in their minds and although there was no sound, could not be any sound, it felt as if their whole being was being shaken by the power of that voice, a voice that was the embodiment of two massive landslides colliding at the bottom of a valley.

You are brave men, the great face said, *I, Korok, admire that. Only courage and fortitude separate us from the beasts and you have much of that. But it will not be enough.*

You can't be Korok! was Jon astounded reply, *he died five hundred years ago!*

Again that terrifying smile.

The version of me made from meat and water is long gone. But my mind, all that was my essence, was digitised and uploaded to the operating system of the Fatal Scimitar. No – I AM the operating system. The Maroun you saw was merely a representation, a shadow play. But I am no puppet. I am Korok and as of now I bring an end to your plans. You will contaminate no more of my soldiers. We will arrive at our destination before long and when my warriors awake they will deal with you in the manner most appropriate to your treachery. Now begone!

And instantly the men's eyes opened as they were flung out of the Educator with such force that Jarz tumbled off his couch.

* * *

After that shock they stood or sat in complete dejection, oppressed with a feeling of utter helplessness.

Jarm said over and over and over again: 'We're all going to die,' until Jon crossed angrily to him and shook him into frightened silence.

Shev stared at Jon. 'It's easy enough to shut him up but what exactly are we able to do here? We're trapped in a vessel of a size we can only guess at with no way of knowing where we are.'

Shana12 suddenly looked up, her face suffused with excitement. 'Jon! I know what the High Official Generation Room is!'

He glared at her, his taut nerves fraying. 'And how does that help us; you know, right here, right now?'

'It doesn't.'

'Then please be quiet Shana.'

Jarz suddenly spoke up from where he had been sitting, crumpled up on the floor.

'We have to go back in.'

'Into the Educator?' Jon demanded, 'No, no, Korok said we wouldn't be allowed back in.'

Jarz looked at them all, one by one.

'What's the alternative? If we can't find our way around this vessel and somehow seize control of it we're finished. As Jarm said, we're all going to die. Once the rest of Korok's army wakes up it'll be over for all of us. We've got to find out where we are on this ship thing.'

'I can't ask you to do that,' Jon said, looking down on the smaller man as he lay huddled on the floor.

'You don't have to,' Jarz said and stood up very slowly. Suddenly he seemed a taller man than he had been before he had sat down. There was determination in his face. Jon was struck, not for the first time, how different this Jarz was from his equivalent on the Hill, once Korok's control was removed.

'I choose to go in.'

None of the others tried to stop him and they watched, almost reverentially, as Jarz lay down on the couch and carefully put the headset on.

At once his eyes closed and his face went blank.

But not for long. Suddenly his face twisted with fear and he cried out in a voice much louder than anyone had thought possible for him: 'No! No!'

Then his body arched until only his feet and shoulders were on the couch. Then he bent the other way so his arms and legs were pointing almost directly at the ceiling.

And so it went on, with opposing muscle groups being stimulated into ever greater contractions. Desperately they tried to hold him down but his tormented musculature was too strong. Each clonic spasm was greater than the previous, eventually sending the women spinning across the room.

Then there was the dreadful sound of bones snapping under the strain. Jarz gave out one last tremendous scream and then all was silence.

The survivors lay where they had been thrown across the room or where they had collapsed near Jarz's corpse.

Eventually Jon raised his head and stared at the body.

That was our last hope, he thought, *Korok has won.*

Seven

Never had Jon felt so utterly helpless, so completely, finally beaten. In his electronic incarnation, Korok had become an all-powerful part of the very ship, a vessel in which they had been reduced to the status of crawling vermin.

They had no weapons; no plans; no hope. And even if they had possessed weapons would good would they do against an enemy that was an intangible essence; an electronic mist that could be anywhere and do anything?

He gave a wry smile: at least if they had had weapons they could kill themselves and cheat Korok of his final triumph by escaping into death.

He looked around; half decided to take that ultimate act. What could be used?

There was nothing in this room.

What about that antechamber, he thought. He remembered the objects he had seen when he and Shana had walked in. Those metal sheets, could they be rolled up and pushed down the throat to cause asphyxia?

It was then an incredible thought hit him almost like a physical blow.

Those things had been in part of the Education Room; ergo, they were tools for learning, for information.

What if those who had designed the *Fatal Scimitar* had planned for a possible problem with the ship's operating system? What if they had stored information in a non-digital, physical form? A form that could be read without software.

It was their only hope. He dragged Shana12 to her feet and ignoring her startled cry pulled her into the antechamber. He spoke to her quickly and quietly; the last thing the others needed was false hope. Once aware of his idea the pair took out a few of the metal sheets and, after some experimentation, slotted them into viewers.

To his incredible joy, the sheets did indeed contain technical data, data which could only be read by biological eyes when in these viewers. Somewhere there must be schematics for the layout of this vessel!

Shana brought the others in and rapidly set them to work, each to a viewer and a stack of the related metal records.

It was a wearisome task. Many times Jon had thought that the next sheet would give him the knowledge he needed. And each time he was disappointed.

And so it went on.

It was Jarm who found it and his cry echoed all around the antechamber and into the main room. Everyone rushed to look over his shoulder and saw a technical blueprint of their vessel and prison; the aptly named *Fatal Scimitar*.

It consisted of a wide cylinder with a great nozzle at one end for expelling the propellant gases. The habitation area was in the mid-section of the cylinder, rotating around the long axis to simulate gravity and as far away as possible from that blazing exhaust. But not too far, for dwarfing all the other structures on the vessel was the great shallow cone of the collecting dish. In operation, a magnetic field would be generated, many dark kilometres across and powerful enough to rip iron from the bodies of any biological entity that got too close.

Using knowledge that only a short time before he had not possessed Jon could see that the hydrogen collected by that great ram scoop would be accelerated by a series of microwave generators and lasers and emerge as a massive thrusting jet, burning outwards at a significant fraction of lightspeed.

Jon's freshly expanded technical knowledge marvelled at the skill which had gone into producing this system; for it was the only feasible way of crossing the tremendous gulfs between the stars without being trapped in a runaway system of demanding

190

ever more fuel to propel ever more mass.

Whatever their undoubted faults, the Protectorate had not lost scientific knowledge.

(Or *was it the slave labour of the Degenerates* a part of his mind wondered.)

But that was not the end of their labours. They still had to find a way to the Control Room and that took almost as long as finding the overall schematic.

But find it they did.

They stood up from their wearisome task and looked at each other. A quiet determination appeared to be radiating from them, almost a tangible aura.

'We all know the way now?' Jon asked, looking at each of the survivors in turn.

They all nodded.

'Then we'll be on our way. But first, an experiment.'

To the others' surprise, Jon crossed to a nearby information screen and activated it.

The unblinking man appeared.

'We want to surrender,' Jon said in a broken voice, 'we've suffered enough. We want assurances we'll be well treated.'

As he had more than half expected the unblinking man's visage disappeared and was replaced by another face.

The flint-like features of an implacable, dark, heavy-boned man.

Korok.

'I am disappointed. Very disappointed,' came that granite voice, 'Disappointed in your weakness and also that you know so little of the Protectorate. It is not those who surrender who obtain our mercy but those who fight to the glorious end.

'Think on that before you surrender.'

The screen went dead.

'Why did you do that?' gasped Jarm, 'You've just made him angry!'

Jon turned. 'I could have taunted him. Threatened him. But this way he thinks we're beaten. It might give us an edge, who knows?'

'We'll certainly need that,' Jorl muttered, 'as all we've got is our fists.'

'No,' Jon said, 'we've got more than that. We've got our brains as well. Come on.'

And with that, they left the Education Room.

* * *

The corridors stretched before them, cold, grey, metallic, slowly curving. Each section looked exactly the same as the previous one. To minds on the edge of abject despair it appeared that their search would never end, *could* never end.

Jon became aware that his Shana was trying to speak to him. He had put Shana36 ahead of him and Shana12 beside him; so worried was he that he might fail to distinguish them. He turned. 'Yes?'

Shana placed her hand on his shoulder, trying to slow his furious march but he did not allow that. They must get to the Control Room!

Shana spoke, breathing heavily as she matched his furious pace. 'The High Official Generation Room – I know what it is.'

'And'

'I didn't have the knowledge before the Educator but now I do. Jon, it's exactly the literal meaning of the words. Korok, Maroun and the rest of them – they're going to come out of it!'

'Nonsense. All we saw were tanks with organic chemicals in them. If they were going to travel on this ship in physical form why wouldn't they be in the pods?'

'Jon, we look human but we're not. We have the bodily shape but our proteins are not natural ones. We were designed to survive a journey of this length – and even then some of us

192

didn't survive, Shev told me. Ordinary humans are not robust enough. They had to find another way.'

'So why not travel as a simpler structure – a collection of zygotes.'

'Anything of great biological complexity would be at risk of degradation in the high energy environment between the stars. But those tanks contain everything that a human body is constructed from, but in the simplest, most radiation-proof form, just the basic molecules, protected by metres of lead shielding. A sophisticated nanotechnology could construct a human body from those compounds once the environment was safe.'

'A body. But only a body. It would know nothing.'

Jon was not looking at Shana otherwise he would have seen her exasperated expression.

'Jon – think! If the consciousness, the memories, the identity can be extracted from a biological brain, digitised and uploaded then the process can be reversed – a digitised mind can be downloaded into a biological brain!'

Jon stopped his mad dash as the full import of her words struck him. The others, suddenly aware that their progress had halted, turned around in puzzlement.

She looked him full in the eye, blue-grey almost on the same level as brown.

'Jon, it would be like they had taken one step on Earth and the next on an alien world. And if they could do it once, they could do it again and again. Jon, this gang of horrors could live as long as the universe!'

Jon stood stock still, staring at Shana; the others gathered around him, anxious to discover what new problem was now facing them. He detailed Shana's revelation to them.

'We must destroy them,' he said slowly, 'even at the cost of our own lives.'

'I don't think so,' Jorl said, 'I'm here to save my life - not throw it away on a theory.'

Jon stared at the cold grey floor, held motionless by indecision. Then he straightened.

'The systems must be programmed to begin regeneration when the ship arrives – at wherever it's going. So we have until then. If we can't control the ship, then they will never come out of those tanks. If we can, then we turn our attention to them after we have made the ship safe.'

The others, even Jorl, nodded in acceptance.

And their journey was resumed.

They noticed that the corridor was becoming wider and the quality of the light was changing, becoming harder, bluer. Arachnoids scurried away from them in all directions.

And then they were there. A great door sensed their approach and slid obediently open.

They came out on a balcony below which stretched banks of humming, buzzing machinery; softly glowing viewer screens; shining, gleaming surfaces everywhere. Here was the home of the arachnoids, for during five hundred long years they had kept the brain of the *Fatal Scimitar* working as well as their programming and dexterity had allowed. The system had been designed as perfectly as human ingenuity could have made it; no possible problem had been unforeseen, uncatered for.

But it had not been enough: the insidious fingers of entropy and a random high-energy event had brought all that brilliant planning to catastrophic failure.

They descended to the main level; slowly, moving like stunned barbarians entering a splendid cathedral of the High Renaissance. They rapidly pooled the knowledge that the Educator had given to them and then Jon approached the largest of the viewer screens, a screen which was wider than the entire astonished group and twice Jon's height.

Instantly it sprang into life. And the image it showed was strangely familiar.

194

It was of a perfectly black background, but not totally black for it was dusted with little lights; little hard, unblinking lights, some noticeably brighter than the others.

Shana grasped his arm. 'Jon – it's my dream. And you saw it too – remember!'

'Yes,' he said, wonderingly, 'when I tried the Hill version of the Educator. I saw this. But now I know what it is.'

'And it is…' Jarm enquired.

For an answer, Shev strode up to the display and, acting on a hunch, held her palm against the screen and flicked it to the right.

The lights in the viewer display suddenly shifted to the right; some disappeared, some came into view.

But something else came into view – a small, painfully bright disc of harsh radiance.

Jon studied the words and numbers that had suddenly flashed across the bottom of the screen.

'G8 main sequence,' he said, apparently to himself. He turned to the others: 'Our destination!'

The others burst into a clamour of excitement, slapping each other on the back and with broad smiles almost splitting their faces. His Shana made as if to kiss him.

But he ignored her and bent down to get a closer look at the numbers and mathematical symbols which were being displayed in a repeating sequence at the bottom of the huge screen. His strong fingers flew back and forth over its lambent surface and he spent quite some time there, staring with slowly narrowing eyes at what they revealed.

Finally he stood upright and turned to look at the group. Jorl took in his expression and snapped: 'Alright – let's have it!'

Jon stared back at his group of comrades, reflecting how they had been flung into an apparently endless maelstrom of danger and trial and how they risen to those challenges with seemingly inexhaustible resources of fortitude.

195

'We have entered this planetary system, just as the Protectorate planned, half a millennium ago. But as Shev told us not long ago, the guidance systems are compromised. We should have begun braking about thirty years ago.

'We did not. We are travelling too fast to be captured by our destination planet. We will describe a hyperbolic arc around this star and then head back out into interstellar space.'

Eight

'Back into interstellar space?' whispered Jarm, 'Then it's all over. We're finished.'

The looks of the faces of his companions told Jon that the opinion was unanimous.

He turned away from them and stared at the glowing instruments. They held the key to controlling the *Fatal Scimitar*; Jon knew that all the technical understanding required to master the vessel was already in his brain – he had just to turn theory into practice and extremely soon.

'All of you!' he shouted in a stentorian roar, 'look at these machines! Find some way of controlling them, operating them! Now!'

For a few moments they just stared at him as if he had suddenly demanded that they learn how to fly but then they realised that he was offering them their only hope of avoiding a slow, cold death between the stars. They all immediately crossed to the machine nearest to them and began examining it; but even in this dreadful emergency Jon kept an eye on the location of Shana36, watching to see if she crossed over 'his" Shana's path. He knew it was irrational, a complete dereliction of duty; a perfect example of failing to get his priorities right.

But he couldn't help it.

It was Shev who found the answer. She pointed at a palm-sized blank pad on the portion of her machine that jutted out to form a kind of shelf or working surface. Tentatively, not daring to hope, she had put her palm on it and a portion of the front of her machine above the working surface had slid upwards and a pair of scalp contacts similar to the Educator pads had slid out.

Jon did the same with his machine with the same result. He pulled the pads out of their recess and stared at them for a few fast-flowing moments. Their resemblance to the Educator pads could not be a coincidence. They must have a similar function, but maybe in reverse – with knowledge flowing from a flesh and blood brain to a machine!

There was a moulded chair in front of every machine and, sitting down, he placed the pads on his scalp.

Instantly a cold mechanical thought that was not his formed in his mind.

Instructions? it said.

Show me all the command instructions.

A great bank of computer commands appeared in his inner vision, rolling inexorably, endlessly upwards to disappear from his purview.

He slowed the display to a more manageable rate and memorised the ten most important ones. The others he could return to later.

He looked over his shoulder to find that his companions had not copied him but stood in an expectant semicircle around him, waiting for something to happen.

No matter. They could learn later, in the meantime…

Activate breaking rockets he commanded into the heart of the great Command Computer.

Activated.

Fire.

Value?

Maximum.

Immediately, instantly, without any delay that human or transhuman senses could have registered, a great roar echoed through the control room; a roar as if a titanic dinosaurian beast was being flayed alive. Contemporaneously there was a great lurch as if the hurtling vessel had hit an obstruction in its headlong flight; an obstruction which slowed the vessel, clung to it like a colossal cephalopod of space, slowing, pulling – but not halting it.

The *Fatal Scimitar* shuddered, jerked, twisted, throwing its inhabitants onto the floor. All around were the terrible sounds of metal straining under enormous forces; great echoing booming noises like distant thunder could be heard crashing and reverberating from all directions.

Jorl got to his feet first. 'The old girl doesn't like it I guess.'

Jon ignored him and resumed his connection with the Control Computer. He called up data on trajectory and velocity and the rates of change of both.

Finally he turned. 'We haven't got a fraction of the power required to establish a stable orbit within this system. We can't make up for thirty years of uninterrupted interstellar velocity in a few hours, days or weeks - even if we had unlimited fuel. We are still on a hyperbolic path.'

'As I believe I said,' Jarm commented, 'we're finished.'

'Possibly not,' was Jon's response, 'we are slowing and there is another way of losing velocity.'

'Reverse slingshot,' Shana36 suddenly interjected.

'Reverse what?' was Jorls's comment as he turned to look at her, 'I must have nodded off in the Educator when they did that one.'

Shana36 ignored him and continued to stare, somewhat unnervingly, at Jon.

'Slingshots or gravitational assists were used in the early days of space probes by using large rotating masses, usually Jupiter, to transfer momentum. However, it's possible to transfer momentum the other way by approaching the object counter to its spin.'

'But the amounts transferred would be minute!,' Shana12 said, who had not failed to notice who her double was staring at.

'Indeed they would,' Jon said, managing not to look directly at either of the women but at a point directly between the Shanas, 'but there are a number of gas giant planets in this system that we can bleed momentum onto. But you're right – it will take a while.'

'Then we'd better get started,' Jon heard Jorl mutter.

'There's a little something we have to do first,' Jon continued, feeling increasingly light-headed as the enormity of what he was about to say started to dominate his mind, 'something that will help us a great deal to shed momentum.'

The others did not rise to the theatricality of his performance and merely waited for him to finish.

'We will pass close to this star on the turning point of our hyperbola and by approaching it correctly we will be able to lose a useful fraction of our momentum,' he finally said.

Jorl turned to look at Shev and then back to Jon.

'That's a rather throwaway remark – "Pass close to the star" – how close?'

'Within zero point one six of an AU.'

The others burst into a confused cacophony of various types of expostulations.

Finally Shana12 asked, 'How hot will it get?'

Jon tried and failed to give a reassuring smile. 'This vessel has a hull designed to withstand half a millennium in interstellar space and the star is cooler than Earth's sun. The maximum temperature on the hull according to the Control Computer – I haven't checked it – will be about 880 kelvins.'

'Hot enough to soften quite a few metals,' Jarm observed mildly, as if he were reading from a technical journal.

'And that's just the heat,' Jorl snapped, 'Surprisingly enough I wasn't asleep during the lecture about hard radiation – Far UV, X-Ray, maybe the occasional gamma ray. Not to mention – but I must – a flood of charged particles shooting through us.'

'I'm afraid there is no alternative,' Jon said, desperately trying to control his growing irritation with Jorl, 'you clearly haven't realised that we have absolutely no way of avoiding the close passage. It's the laws of gravity that have made this choice for us – not me. But if we control our path we can use it to our advantage.'

'If we survive!' Jorl growled, looking at the others.

Jon nodded calmly. 'If we survive.'

* * *

The days passed as the starship continued its ineluctable fall towards the dread fusion furnace which formed the centre of this alien planetary system. The image of that inferno was noticeably larger each time anyone dared to look at it. Gradually more and more details could be made out on its surface; great sunspot clusters - the smallest of which was larger than the planet Earth - became easily visible. On the limbs, pale pink tongues of prominences could be seen reaching out into the blackness of space, looking like the delicate feathery fronds of some strange plant of fire but in reality great towers of plasma, hundreds of kilometres high.

And the heat. At first it was not noticeable as the synthetic humans busied themselves learning every aspect of the great starship, learning every nuance of the control commands, teaching themselves how the various systems functioned together.

But there came a day when the heat could no longer be ignored, when the rivulets of sweat had to be brushed away from eyes every few seconds. Like an invisible predator it stalked them, sapping their determination, their drive, their self-belief, sucking away their strength and energy.

Clothes were soon discarded but with nude bodies glistening with sweat, they worked on. Enormous quantities of water were consumed and expelled but they could only force themselves to eat small amounts of solid food.

The arachnoids ferried them a continuous supply of anti-radiation drugs.

Working together, Shev and Jon found that the vessel had

the facility to produce a cloaking magnetic field which would deflect the star's terrible torrent of charged particles by forming a miniature magnetosphere. But the controlling software had been corrupted during the cosmic ray burst. Doggedly, line by line, they reconstructed the code which would allow it to flash into existence. Line by line they worked, snapping and snarling at each other in their exhaustion; huge drops of sweat falling steadily over their work, blurring and smearing the symbols. After many weary hours they could do no more: either it would work or they would die.

Jon sent the command.

It worked.

'Neutrons will still get through,' Shev observed gloomily.

'So they will,' was Jon's only reply and then he turned to the next problem.

The heat intensified.

Jarm and the Shanas discovered stores of lead-based creams with which the team liberally plastered themselves, turning them into ghastly white spectres.

'Isn't lead poisonous?' enquired Shana36 with mock innocence.

'So is hard radiation!' was the other Shana's response.

The heat intensified.

The air became blisteringly hot and the metal surfaces painful to touch. Under the lead paint skin began to crack and blister. Each breath brought burning air into their lungs. They shielded their eyes from penetrant radiation with lead infused visors that threw everything into a grey twilight.

Even the simplest task required great effort, both physical and mental. Still they worked at the controls, feeling the shifting gravitational and electromagnetic forces trying to twist the starship's path into one that terminated in the photosphere. They took it in turns to attempt to sleep on the hot metal floor while those awake battled with the forces which hungrily, mockingly

202

tried to pull them into a fiery death.

At one point Jorl stood up. 'I'm going to that Regeneration Room you told me about. The shielding is heavier there. I'm not going to stay here and be cooked alive! If you've got any sense you'll come with me,' with the last comment being directed to the team other than Jon.

The latter stood up and barred his way. 'You're going nowhere. We need everyone here, manning the controls. We can't allow anyone to become a passenger.'

Jorl stared at him. 'We? You mean "you", don't you? Actually, I don't remember anyone voting for you in the election. In truth, I don't even remember the election!'

Jon did not move. He stood stock-still on the rocking, shuddering floor of the Control Room.

'Jorl if I have to knock you out I will. But that means we'll lose your abilities at the controls. So I'd rather not do it. Don't make me do it.'

The two men remained staring at each other for some time with the others having turned in their seats to watch the outcome. Finally, Jorl gave a short nod and slowly went back to his machine.

The star had now filled the entirety of the viewscreen which had automatically stepped the blinding glare down by many orders of magnitude. Still it blazed like a sea of molten steel, so close now that only the edge of one sunspot was visible.

The creaking and groaning of the ship's fabric had blurred together into one continuous roar.

The heat intensified.

And so it was that the entire group had collapsed into unconsciousness as the ship rounded the turning point of the dreadful hyperbola and began its retreat from the thwarted star.

* * *

203

Gradually Jon became aware of his surroundings. His first sensation was of a terrible, oppressive heat that lay over him in a suffocating blanket; then he was aware that the deck below him was shaking and jerking as if in the jaws of a tremendous beast and finally he could hear an all-pervasive roar. A sound, he eventually realised, of great engines performing at the very peak of their tolerances.

He rolled over and slowly pushed himself up so he was resting on his palms and knees. He looked around and saw his companions lying in various positions on the metal floor; some on their backs, some on their fronts, some in a foetal position. To his great relief, he could just make out through the hurricane of noise that they were starting to make sounds of awakening. And slowly, one by one, they did.

For some time they said nothing; did nothing, just showing simple relief for having survived the close encounter with the system's star; having survived the turning of the deadly hyperbola.

Hour by hour the temperature dropped.

Hour by hour the throats of the braking rockets blazed white-hot as they fought the implacable equation of momentum.

Hour by hour the thunder of the mighty task of those tortured engines rolled through the ship.

Finally Jon said after studying the diagnostics on his viewscreen: 'We can't maintain this expenditure of energy. We'll have no fuel for manoeuvring among the giant planets. We'll have to cut the thrust.'

He studied the scrolling numbers on the screen while the others waited; waited to hear what existential issue now awaited them. They stood there like wraiths or spectres, still clad in peeling anti-radiation paint, which in several places did not cover weeping blisters.

'There's been a significant change in our trajectory. The curve we're following is now at least parabolic, possibly even elliptical,' Jon finally announced.

Shana12's face lit up. 'An ellipse! That's a closed curve. It means we'll come back to this system!'

Jon gave her a grave glance. 'I said it might be an ellipse. And even under the most optimistic assumptions it would take us out to about a parsec at apastron. I'll leave you to calculate how long it would take us to get back.'

The little sparks of joy flickered out immediately and their usual expressions of stolid acceptance returned.

Jon stood silent for a moment, staring at his companions, wondering at their reserves of strength and silently cursing the authors of all this suffering – the now incredibly distant Protectorate. But no! – he checked himself: The Protectorate was not distant; it was with them in an invisible form. Somewhere in the Artificial Intelligence that ran this vessel, at the centre of its intangible web, lurked another intelligence – Korok. They could never relax, never declare victory while that threat remained. In any electron flow Korok could be there; hiding in the voltages, secreting himself in the amperages. He had not moved against them, Jon knew, because all they had done had been to preserve the *Fatal Scimitar* and thus the Protectorate's original plan.

But should they do anything to prevent that plan...

Jon knew that there could be no safety until Korok was finally confronted.

And destroyed.

Nine

The main drive had been shut off leaving the starship to sweep through space in unpowered freefall and the consequent silence felt strange, eerie, as if something had gone terribly amiss. Ears used to a solid wall of thunderous sound found it hard to adjust to the relative quiet.

Only relative quiet, of course. The fabric of the ship had suffered greatly in the close passage and it was still groaning as the stresses and strains gradually worked their way out. Many bulkheads had failed and the travellers could see on their viewers that the entire vessel was swarming with over-worked arachnoids desperately trying to close tears and rips in the structure while being showered by fountains of sparks.

It was odd to be safe from imminent danger and actually to find themselves with very little to do. To conserve energy, the ship was now on a Hohmann transfer orbit out to the realm of the giant planets of the alien system; the course had been set and the ship's control systems were perfectly adequate to maintain that course.

But Jon had something to show them. He called them over to the huge wall viewer and pointed to a dim star-like spark in the blackness. He placed a finger on it and the spark vanished temporarily.

'That is the destination that the Protectorate set half a millennium ago. That is the terrestrial planet that we are meant to land on and subjugate.'

'Subjugate?' Jarm enquired, 'Are there any signs of a civilisation on that body?'

'None whatsoever,' Jon replied, 'The Protectorate may have been guilty of a little wishful thinking. But that was only the first plan: if the planet was found to be uninhabited then it was our job to engineer it so a second Protectorate could be established on it. Which would in time fight the first.'

'How sweet,' Shana36 commented, 'so some of the tubes in the Regeneration Room must be intended for female resurrections. I doubt if *we* would be allowed to breed once our use was over.'

'Of course. The resurrection process can be run any number of times with slight alterations each time to avoid inbreeding. And of course, there would be far more females than males.'

'Probably the only males would be the High Officials themselves,' Jorl grinned, 'Boy, will they be busy!'

'Yes,' Jon replied, thinking it was time he let up on Jorl somewhat, 'but someone will have to do it!'

The group broke up then but Jon took Shev aside and they went off together and started working on some project on the Command Computer.

They worked together for many hours. Shana12 observed them for afar with gradually narrowing eyes. She had enquired once as to whether she could help and Shev had simply replied with a brusque "No." Shana had on one occasion almost shared her disquiet with Shana36 but at the last moment, she had thought that maybe that was a confidence too far to share with her double.

Eventually she heard Jon say 'That's it! It's in place!' with a clear note of triumph. Shev looked pleased too and the duo went their separate ways.

'What was all that about?' Shana asked, when she finally got Jon on his own.

He smiled and said: 'Something very dear to your heart. But I'm not going to say anything out loud. We think that we're alone in this room but we're not. If I'm right we'll all find out when the time comes.'

Days passed as the ship flew silently on through the indifferent darkness. The terrible heat drained away until the time

207

came when with great satisfaction they were able to put their clothes back on – though only after both clothes and bodies had undergone an extremely thorough wash.

The scene on the great viewer did not change to any significant degree: they were still months away from their first encounter with a giant planet.

Then Jon called them all together.

To their surprise, he gave them all small writing pads made of paper.

He wrote something down on his pad and passed it to the nearest member of the group.

Each member in turn read the following message: 'It is time to destroy the Regeneration Chamber.'

The others stared at him in surprise and not a little trepidation.

This was the long-expected move against Korok: this would be the final test that they would face. If they lost it would be all over for them.

How? Jarm wrote.

We need weapons, was Jon's written reply.

The group sat silently for a while. Weapons? Where could they find weapons?

Then Jorl laughed and spent some time writing. He passed the result straight to Jon.

Jon are you sure you want to be our leader? We were meant to conquer a world. There must be weapons on the ship!

Jon gave a smile which was twisted with embarrassment. *Of course!* he thought, *I must be slipping.*

He nodded to Shev and they both lift the group but continued to communicate by writing on the pads.

We must locate them without alerting Korok, he wrote.

Yes, she wrote, *we'll have to search using machine code only.*

And when we find them – we move fast.

Of course was the reply.

They returned to the group and Jon wrote a detailed description of what they would do when they had weapons. They nodded in silent acquiescence.

They stood up, burned all the papers.

And waited.

* * *

The location and password were displayed on Jon's viewer. Instantly he memorised it and deleted it.

He stood up. *What were the resources of the creature he was up against?* he asked himself for the thousandth time.

A biological brain was being emulated on superbly constructed software. Korok had been a soldier – could he see that the software of which he was himself a part was being used against him?

There was no point in speculating. They would find out soon enough.

Now they must move – and fast.

They formed into a tight group with Jon at their head and left the Control Room.

The interstellar ramjet hurtled onwards; oblivious of their departure, staying true to its preordained path.

Down they went; one level down; two levels down.

Then a great door made of case-hardened steel. And a pad by its side.

The pad was pressed.

The password was given.

The door opened.

Inside were row after row of automatic weapons, stretching deep into the interior of the ship. There were revolver types, rifle types, machine guns. In the dim distance could be seen wheeled and tracked vehicles. It was an arsenal of every type of projectile throwing armament known to the Protectorate!

The nearest rows held automatic rifles and magazine clips; devices of death that had been put there half a millennium earlier in the sure and certain hope that they would be used in anger!

And so they would.

They took them; they took grenades; they took plastic explosives.

They climbed back up the levels they had descended, up seemingly endless metal stairs. There were elevators but Jon did not want to find that a door which had closed behind him would no longer open. Even now Korok must be aware that something not in the plan was happening.

They found the High Official Generator Room and to Jon's surprise he found that the password had not been changed. He had been prepared to blast his way in with explosive charges.

The outer door and the inner door opened before them.

It was as Jon and Shana remembered, row after row of transparent cylinders filled with a milky, slowly stirring liquid; tall tubes stretching into gloomy obscurity, with four standing out in a separate row.

Jon felt that there was no longer any need for silence.

'Shoot them!' he yelled, 'Now!'

It was then that the bulkhead next to them, weakened by the endless flexing and bending that it had endured in the stellar encounter, decided to give way. With a terrible blast of screams of tortured metal tearing, a great, jagged hole appeared within which electrical arcs crackled and danced, striking this way and that like blazing serpents.

The intruders were flung to the floor, the weapons falling from their grasp.

As they lay there stunned and dazed they saw mechanical legs approaching and, sitting up, found themselves surrounded by the arachnoid guardians of the Room. They stared at disc-shaped bodies supported by spindly legs and found ruby-coloured eyes staring back at them. And they also saw various unpleasant jointed appendages being extended towards them.

'You are too close to the Generation Tubes,' a thin voice intoned, 'You may not approach within two metres.'

Jon stared at the creature standing over him. It was illuminated by leaping arcs of electrical death that were darting and flashing in all directions. Sooner or later one of them would strike either him or the creature.

But he could not wait.

He rolled over and grasped the automatic rifle which had fallen from his fingers, lifted it with trembling hands and fired.

The creature disintegrated into little flying pieces of metal accompanied by blinding electrical shorts that added to the hellish mayhem into which the Generation Room had descended. The flashes of the bolts of electricity seeking to ground themselves produced a dizzying, stroboscopic effect as the others staggered to their feet and unleashed a salvo of bullets on the guardian arachnoids. One by one they approached, uttering the same warning and one by one they were blown apart. Choking smoke and metallic dust filled the room, stinging eyes already half-blinded by the hissing electric arcs.

Jon tried to gather his forces again and raised his voice as high as he could so the others could hear him above the electrical hurricane.

'Shoot the cylinders! The cylinders!'

But they did not.

They stood motionless in grotesque rigidity as horror seized their muscles, their volition.

A section of wall had slid open and something had emerged.

Something that looked like an arachnoid but one designed and built by a crazed sadist.

It stood nearly three metres tall topped by an elliptical head with two large crimson eyes. And coming from its torso were four arms giving it the impression of a mechanical imagining of a Hindu god.

But if it was a god, it was a god of death for each arm terminated in some kind of blade. Blades that were whirling; blades that were cutting across each other like those of huge scissors. Blades that would inflict sudden death or endless pain.

Then came a voice. Unlike the simple arachnoids this head had jaws which moved as the words were uttered.

And the voice was like the sound of great boulders, smashing each other into splinters.

'I am the Lord Korok,' the metal head said, 'I am very pleased by your fighting spirit. You have given me great sport. I have of course been fully aware of all your plans despite your childish efforts at subterfuge but I needed you to stabilise the flight of this vessel. That is now done.

'But I must move on now to new challenges. And I must now kill you.'

No-one moved. Totally awed they simply looked up at the metal monstrosity that was about to kill them.

Then Jon shook off the fear that this thing had engendered. He remembered all that had happened on the Hill under Korok's rule. He remembered the horrific death of Jarz51.

And hatred replaced fear.

'Korok!' he cried, 'you have not won and you cannot win. Shev and I found the code that creates your self-awareness, your consciousness, the emulation of the original Korok. And we firewalled it off from the basic part of the ship's operating system. Now you've downloaded your mind into this machine the version of you that is in there is the only one with volition. The original of you is imprisoned in the Control Computer, in solitary confinement, unable to act. Only observe.

'And when this copy is deleted – so are you.'

The Korok machine was silent and motionless for a few moments.

Jon knew that he was trying to communicate with the original version of himself in the Control Computer.

212

But there would be no reply – he and Shev had seen to that.

Suddenly the thing lurched forward with arms outstretched.

'Clever. But the cowardly way of the Degenerate – I had expected better. Now die like a Degenerate.'

Together the entire group fired their automatic weapons in a single thunderous fusillade at their terrible enemy. Every bullet found its mark: the head, the torso, the arms; Korok shuddered and swayed under that relentless storm of impacts but still he came on. Spent bullets ricocheted in all directions, rebounding from the walls, plunging into the hissing electrical arcs to be volatilised.

Towering over Jon, Korok flicked his gun away as if it were a matchstick and picked him up with sharp metal fingers. He held him dangling there for some moments so Jon was forced to stare into hellish crimson eyes and then Korok flung him against a wall. Jon felt the lower part of his left leg snap an instant before his lacerated body crashed to the floor.

Korok whirled around to face the others and made two steps towards them. Where he lay Jon could see the two Shanas, Shev and Jarm through the swirling blue-grey smoke, looking like helpless mannequins below the metal monstrosity. Jorl was nowhere to be seen.

Korok lifted one leg to step over a mass of disintegrated arachnoids.

And Jarm and the Shanas acted as one and leapt for that leg as the creature was momentarily unbalanced.

Korok was flung backwards, lost his balance completely and in a whirling pirouette he went down - into the most massive of the crackling, darting electric arcs. It encased his entire form in blue, leaping discharges, sending black smoke curling upwards from his joints.

And also convulsed and charred the body of one of the Shanas whom he had grabbed as he fell.

No! Jon screamed inwardly, *Shana! Which Shana were you!*

213

After it was finally certain that Korok would move no more, they came to Jon and using two of the automatic rifles they splinted his broken leg. They could do nothing for the cuts but transhumans heal quickly.

Shana stood over him and kissed him.

Who are you? he thought, *who are you!*

They took him to the charred body of the other Shana and he looked down on the carbonised thing, still with little wisps of grey smoke rising from it. Surely no-one had ever faced a situation like this before, grieving for his lost love when, perhaps, she was standing next to him, alive, vibrant, triumphant.

Who are you ! he thought to himself, *who are you?*

They soon found a way of discharging the contents of the cylinders into space and did that for the first four. The others could wait.

Thus the substances which could have been made into new bodies for Gang Jianguo, Rocha, Maroun and Korok became insignificant components of the interplanetary medium.

They then took Jon back to the Control Room, passing hordes of arachnoids toiling to heal the *Fatal Scimitar*, and Jon began his own healing.

But one question kept burning in his mind.

EPILOGUE

Jon and Shana stood side by side on the hillside looking out over the domes of the new settlement.

Time had not touched them very severely as yet, even though it had taken eight wearisome years of shuttling back and forth between the giant planets before sufficient velocity had been shed in order for them to establish a stable orbit around the system's one terrestrial planet.

At that thought, Jon looked up into the darkening purple sky. There he saw, as he had known he would, a small point of light moving slowly against the real stars.

The *Fatal Scimitar* still faithfully circling their new home, still following the same endless path after all these years. They could have renamed it of course, from the name Korok had given it but what would have been the point? – it would never travel between the stars again.

They stood there as the sky gradually darkened and the purple began to shade slowly into black. No more would they see monochrome crimson or viridian skies – for their new home had many features similar to distant Earth and its skies were full of endless variety: swelling cumulus clouds; wispy cirrus; towering cumulonimbus, rain, hail, lightning but also many days of gentle blue skies and kindly warm breezes.

No more would they wield sharp swords in strong hands and bring evil creatures their just rewards.

Shana glanced at Jon. He had aged but only in the slow, forgiving way that transhumans did. His muscles had lost some of their tone and his centre of gravity had moved slightly downward. But he was still Jon.

Jon glanced at Shana. Thin vertical lines had started to form on her upper lip and her mass of amber-gold hair held one pure white hair. But her bosom was still reasonably horizontal – no mean feat given that their new home's gravity was almost twice that of Earth's. The children had adapted well and showed no conditions which could be traced to this world's heavier pull.

Many of the sleepers in the stasis pods had not survived the close passage of the star but enough had so that they were a population large enough to form a viable society and, finally purged of Korok's conditioning, those survivors had disembarked from the circling starship. And had begun the Herculean task of moulding an alien world to be a fit home for their kind.

But Jon still found that once in a while his thoughts turned from those great endeavours to a question much closer to his immediate concerns.

Jon was reasonably sure which of the two Shanas stood by his side, her hand in his.

He had never asked the questions which would have put the matter beyond doubt and Shana had never offered to answer them.

'If you love me then you would never ask,' she had said once.

And so he never had.

But he still went on an annual pilgrimage up into the higher hills to stand before a small cairn. The largest stone in the front of the cairn bore the single word: SHANA.

There was much to do; this world was not Earth and was still hostile in many ways. The Protectorate's hopes had been unfulfilled: the planet had not borne an alien civilisation ripe for conquest and enslavement. Indeed it had been completely lifeless until the settlers had descended from the starship.

So much to do, so much to do. The ground had to be seeded with such things as nitrogen-fixing bacteria; soil producing invertebrates had to be introduced. It would be many centuries before the world would become a garden.

And there were other problems: This planetary system was

216

younger than Sol's and was still full of planetoidal debris that could destroy any nascent civilisation. They would have to be dealt with soon.

But once again Jon had other things on his mind.

'We cannot allow the Protectorate to expand into the galaxy,' he finally said, almost to himself.

'You mean we must set up a quarantine around the Solar system,' Shana said, slightly hopefully.

'No,' was Jon's grim reply, 'we can't englobe the entire Solar system. The volume is too great for any resources we are likely to have for many centuries. Something would slip through. We will have to go all the way to Earth itself.'

Shana looked alarmed. 'But why Jon? There can't be anything left of the Degenerates after all this time. There's no-one to rescue!'

Jon shook his head. 'No Shana. Any tyranny needs an underclass to despise and terrorise. There'll be something of them remaining, even if they have forgotten who they once were, what they once had and how they lost it when they beat the last of their swords into a ploughshare. Soon we will be able to cross the distance to Earth in a tenth of the time we took to get here. One day the Protectorate, or their slave scientists, will discover the same process. With that power, true imperialism can begin. So we have to make the Protectorate discover that they too can be conquered.'

Shana touched his arm so he turned and looked her full in the face.

(*Who are you?* he thought.)

'What then Jon? We hold down a conquered population of billions forever?'

'No,' said Jon and his words were like iron, 'Homo sapiens has had its chance. It had many periods of lucidity, of greatness but it always relapsed. The human nervous system ultimately proved incapable of holding the necessary qualities of true

217

civilisation for long enough for them to become irreversible. Ages of light always collapsed into darkness.'

Shana held his arm tighter. Her face was tense in the deepening twilight.

'But Jon, think of Classical Greece, the Compassionate Buddha, Leonardo da Vinci. All that they achieved as they struggled up from savagery.'

Jon shook his head. 'No – those times never lasted; the species couldn't maintain the level of integration required to sustain those societies. Humanity was trapped in a cave of shadows by its limitations; most humans could see that a better civilisation was possible; they could strive towards that goal and occasionally reach it for a few precious moments but always it would slip from their grasp. They have shown over and over that they cannot manage their own affairs; neither can an outside force save them. There will always be another Korok.'

Shana recoiled. 'You mean genocide!'

Jon shook his head again; his face becoming infinitely sad. Soon it would be too dark to discern his features.

'No, it will be a peaceful, managed decline. But one that cannot be reversed. Some will know that it is happening but they will accept that nothing in the universe is built for eternity. We will ensure that they are as happy as possible as the end of their story approaches. Finally they will be happy, I promise.'

He turned from Shana and looked up at the stars, now appearing in their multitudes in a black sky. He selected one undistinguished point of light from among the host upon which to rest his gaze.

'And peace?' said Shana in the darkness.

'Yes,' Jon replied, with a deep sadness in his voice, 'Peace. After so much suffering we will give them that.'

THE END